"Are you hurt?" N

Only in her heart. Her
hurt."

"That's good," he said. "Now I want you to give me that knife."

She nodded at him and handed him the blade. The chill sank deeper into her flesh, into her bones. She thought she was safe here, but everything was falling apart, brick by brick.

"Nicole."

At the sound of her name, she started as if waking from an endless nightmare.

"I need to take care of you before I do anything else," he said, holding out his hand toward her. Dumbly, she stared at the very masculine appendage, all muscle and tendon. Her gaze lifted to his face. His high cheekbones, dark brown eyes and well-tanned complexion hinted at Native American heritage.

"Come on," he urged. "Take my hand. You're going to be okay."

She pulled herself up and slumped against him. His kindness stirred the lonely emptiness inside her. A tear spilled down her cheek as she buried her face against his coat. It would be so good to have someone to lean on, someone she could trust.

Dear Harlequin Intrigue Reader,

Those April showers go hand in hand with a welcome downpour of gripping romantic suspense in the Harlequin Intrigue line this month!

Reader-favorite Rebecca York returns to the legendary 43 LIGHT STREET with *Out of Nowhere*—an entrancing tale about a beautiful blond amnesiac who proves downright lethal to a hard-edged detective's heart. Then take a detour to New Mexico for *Shotgun Daddy* by Harper Allen—the conclusion in the MEN OF THE DOUBLE B RANCH trilogy. In this story a Navajo protector must safeguard the woman from his past who is nurturing a ticking time bomb of a secret.

The momentum keeps building as Sylvie Kurtz launches her brand-new miniseries—THE SEEKERS—about men dedicated to truth, justice…and protecting the women they love. But at what cost? Don't miss the debut book, *Heart of a Hunter,* where the search for a killer just might culminate in rekindled love. Passion and peril go hand in hand in *Agent Cowboy* by Debra Webb, when COLBY AGENCY investigator Trent Tucker races against time to crack a case of triple murder!

Rounding off a month of addictive romantic thrillers, watch for the continuation of two new thematic promotions. A handsome sheriff saves the day in *Restless Spirit* by Cassie Miles, which is part of COWBOY COPS. *Sudden Recall* by Jean Barrett is the latest in our DEAD BOLT series about silent memories that unlock simmering passions.

Enjoy all of our great offerings.

Sincerely,

Denise O'Sullivan
Senior Editor
Harlequin Intrigue

RESTLESS SPIRIT
CASSIE MILES

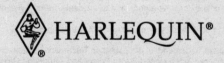

HARLEQUIN®

TORONTO • NEW YORK • LONDON
AMSTERDAM • PARIS • SYDNEY • HAMBURG
STOCKHOLM • ATHENS • TOKYO • MILAN • MADRID
PRAGUE • WARSAW • BUDAPEST • AUCKLAND

ISBN 0-373-22769-8

RESTLESS SPIRIT

Copyright © 2004 by Kay Bergstrom

Visit us at www.eHarlequin.com

Printed in U.S.A.

ABOUT THE AUTHOR

From the balcony of her high-rise, Cassie Miles has a view of the gold dome of the Colorado State Capitol and the front range of the Rockies. If she could find a way to add the ocean, she'd have the best of all possible worlds. The southern Colorado setting for *Restless Spirit* is a fascinating area with spectacular vistas and a strong Native American influence from the nearby Ute Mountain, Navajo and Hopi reservations.

Recently voted Writer of the Year by Rocky Mountain Fiction Writers, Cassie attends critique groups specializing in mystery and in romance, the perfect balance for Harlequin Intrigue books. One of her daughters once described her writing this way, "Romantic suspense. You know, kiss-kiss, bang-bang." If only it were that simple.

Books by Cassie Miles

†Colorado Search and Rescue

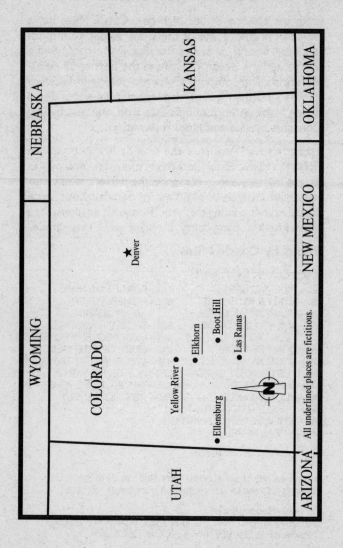

WYOMING

NEBRASKA

UTAH

COLORADO

• Yellow River

★ Denver

Elkhorn

• Ellensburg

• Boot Hill

• Las Ranas

N

KANSAS

OKLAHOMA

ARIZONA   NEW MEXICO

All underlined places are fictitious.

CAST OF CHARACTERS

Nicole Ferris—A waitress at the Elkhorn Cafe. She's on the run from big cities and dark secrets in her childhood and not-so-distant past.

Mace Sheridan—Sheriff of Sterling County, Colorado. Half Ute and half rancher, he feels responsible for all the folks in his county.

Joey Wentworth—Nicole's roommate is an irresponsible artist who helped Nicole when she needed a friend.

Blake Wentworth—Joey's uncle is CEO of Wentworth Oil Exploration.

Luke Heflin—The special agent for the FBI takes over jurisdiction in the Elkhorn crimes.

Barry Thompson—Mace's dispatcher and former partner is a computer whiz.

Don Blackbird—A local man who knows some of Joey's secrets.

Jewel Sheridan—Mace's sister would like to see her big brother settle down.

Derek Brewer—A wealthy Denver attorney who married Nicole as a trophy.

Chapter One

The little blue Ford Escort sputtered and died.

Nicole Ferris coasted the car to a stop on the shoulder. Her headlights shone on a two-lane black asphalt road that sliced through snow-dusted fields and disappeared into the mountains.

She pumped the gas pedal and cranked the ignition. "Come on, baby. You can do it."

The Escort coughed, but the engine didn't catch. In the glow of the dashboard lights, Nicole read the gas gauge. Empty? But that was impossible! Yesterday there was half a tank, and she hadn't gone anywhere but to work and back. How could she be riding on empty?

Realization dawned like a slap in the face. "Joey," she said.

This morning, Joey had borrowed her car to use while his BMW was getting an oil change. Joey Wentworth, her roommate, must have run her car completely out of gas. Damn his inconsiderate hide! She could just kill him!

This wasn't the first time—not even the second or the third time—that he'd shown himself to be an irresponsible, spoiled-brat, wannabe-artist, rich kid. But what could she do? Nicole couldn't break up with Joey, because he wasn't her boyfriend, only a roomie. She couldn't throw him out, because his family owned the cabin where they lived.

The solution was to pack her bags and move on, but the thought exhausted her. Staying here—in godforsaken Elkhorn, Colorado—was a hundred times better than being on the run again.

Resigned, she cut the headlights, twisted her key from the ignition and stepped outside into the freezing cold. She started walking.

There were no phone booths, no taxis, not even an errant pickup truck. It was after eleven o'clock and nobody else was out this late on a weeknight in October, nobody but Nicole, and she was nothing more than a speck in this vast, vacant, southern Colorado landscape—a pathetic little speck wearing a red parka over her pink tunic and slacks uniform that was wilted and wrinkled after an eight-hour shift at the Elkhorn Café where the specialty of the house was fried. Fried potatoes. Fried chicken. Fried bread. After working there for five months, the stench of deep-fat grease clung to her skin, her clothes and her long blond braid.

Peering through the desolate dark, she estimated it was only three miles to the cabin, but she was already chilled. And tired. And hungry. There hadn't been time to eat during the hectic Monday-night football game with the Broncos on television.

They'd lost. Twenty-four to sixteen. And she took their defeat personally. *Losers! We're all losers on a cold night when sunrise is nothing more than a distant unbelievable promise.* She had to keep slogging onward. Icy wetness seeped inside her sneakers. Her clammy socks twined around her toes as she trudged down the winding dirt road that was half frozen and half slush.

Finally she saw the light from the kitchen window of their cabin. Joey's BMW was parked under a stand of Ponderosa pines, which meant he was here—warm and cozy and unaware of the inconvenience he'd caused her.

Yanking her keys from her purse, Nicole hurried toward the red-trimmed log cabin. But there was no need to unlock the door. It stood slightly ajar, letting the heat escape. How typically wasteful! How typically Joey! She marched inside. "Joey, you little creep! You—"

Her voice echoed in the L-shaped living room. She hit the switch by the door. The overhead light shone on chaos. The bookshelves were pulled down, coffee tables overturned, magazines and books scattered all over the place. The sofa lay on its back. The logs by the moss-rock fireplace were strewn like spilled matchsticks. The TV and VCR sat in the middle of the braided oval area rug.

They'd been robbed! But why was the television set here? Were the robbers still in the house?

Nicole listened hard. She heard nothing but the sound of her own labored breathing.

She ought to run to the neighbor's, but nobody lived nearby. The cabins in this area were usually vacant in winter. And Joey's car was parked out front. He might still be in the house. The robbers might have hurt him, left him unconscious. She had to find him. "Joey? Are you here?"

Stepping over a pile of shredded magazines and a sofa pillow that had been slashed open to expose the white batting, Nicole edged toward the kitchen, ready to pivot and run if she encountered anyone.

The kitchen had not been disturbed. The tile countertops shone clean and tidy. The only mess came from her own muddy footprints on the patterned linoleum floor.

She tore open a drawer and pulled out a carving knife to use as a weapon. Holding the steel blade in front of her, she lifted the receiver from the wall phone and punched in the emergency numbers.

After three rings, a male voice answered, "Dispatch."

"Is this 9-1-1?"

"Sure is. What's the problem?"

"This is Nicole Ferris. I live at the Wentworth cabin, and I'm—" She was scared and angry. Hot and cold at the same time. She'd felt this way so many times before. A terrible apprehension crawled up her spine.

"Is this Nicole from the café?" the dispatcher asked.

"We've been robbed." She fought the quaver in her voice. "Everything's torn apart."

"Calm down," he said. "Is anybody hurt?"

"I don't know."

"Is someone there with you?"

"I don't think so." The cabin *felt* empty. "Should I look around?"

"Don't go anywhere. Give me your address."

"Seven-three-three-seven Coyote Road."

"Stay on the line," he ordered. "I'm calling the sheriff."

Over the open phone line, she heard the dispatcher's mumbled conversation. He must have been listening to a country-western radio station because, in the background, she also heard the classic Patsy Cline song, "Who's Sorry Now?"

I am. She shuddered. What if this vandalism wasn't the work of robbers? *What if Derek had found her?*

A sob caught in the back of her throat. She'd escaped from her husband, had fled from him, hidden from him. She couldn't face Derek again, couldn't stand up to his abuse. *Oh God, what if he'd been here?* What if he'd found Joey and punished him?

Her anxiety heightened. She had to protect Joey. He wasn't big or tough. He was sensitive. An artist. Though his behavior was annoying and immature, she thought of him as the younger brother she never had.

"Nicole, I'm back," the dispatcher said. "The sheriff is on his way. You're going to be okay."

"I've got to look for Joey."

"Don't hang up," he said. "Nicole, this is Barry Thompson. You've seen me at the café. I wear glasses."

Wire-rimmed glasses, a shiny bald head and a beard. "I know who you are."

"I want you to stay on the phone and look around. Tell me what you see."

She glanced toward the door that led from the kitchen to the back porch. It was still locked with the dead bolt in place.

"Nicole? Are you there?"

"The back door is locked."

Barry asked, "What else do you see?"

She couldn't stand here answering irrelevant questions. She had to search for Joey. "I'll be right back."

"Nicole, no! Don't—"

She placed the telephone receiver on the countertop. Gripping her knife, she left the kitchen and sidled through the front room.

In her small bedroom at the front of the cabin, the drawers had been yanked open. Her bed covers were torn apart. Her jewelry box on the dresser was empty, which was no big deal. She didn't own any valuable gems. Not anymore.

Then she saw something else that made her heart sink: a cigar box with an ornate picture of an Aztec princess on the top. The box was usually tucked into the bottom of her hamper under her dirty clothes which were now strewn around the room. In that cigar box, she kept her cash money. Nearly two thousand dollars, it was every hard-earned penny she'd saved since moving to Elkhorn. It was empty. "Damn it!"

Leaving her bedroom, she crept down the hall past the bathroom and stood outside the door to Joey's combination bedroom and art studio. Though she occasionally posed for him, she never entered this spacious room without his permission. This was his domain. "Joey? Are you in there?"

Her palms were sweating. The knife handle felt slick in her grasp. With her left hand, she twisted the knob, pushed the door open, reached inside and turned on the light.

At first glance the clutter in his studio seemed orderly. Art supplies were scattered over built-in countertops. Long-handled brushes stuck out of glass jars. A whiff of turpentine scented the air. Canvases were stacked against the walls beneath the multipaned windows. Joey's unmade bed in the corner of the room mocked her. He should have been sleeping there, blithely ignoring the fact that he'd run her car out of gas.

She crossed the gray-tiled floor, which was marked with an unsymmetrical pattern of spills and splatters in myriad shades of green and gold and purple and red. A dark, rich blood-red.

Near the center of the room, there were fresh smears, as if someone had walked through a puddle dragging his heels. Nicole hoped it was only paint, only a splash of red pigment on the floor.

Drawn toward the crimson splotch, she squatted, then knelt. Her sense of balance was shaky. When she reached down, her fingers shook. The instant she touched the red daubs on the floor, she knew it was blood.

Nauseated, she wiped the visceral liquid from her fingertips, leaving prints on the floor. Her gaze circled the studio, taking in several landscape paintings. Sunrise over Sleeping Squaw Mountain. The churning rapids of the Dolores River. Clouds above sagebrush. And a portrait.

When she stood, she felt dizzy. As if walking a tightrope, she approached the acrylic painting of a woman with a long blond braid. The background was a cemetery populated by devils. In the foreground, Nicole recognized her own blue eyes and her wide, unsmiling mouth. Below her collarbone, he'd painted away the skin, exposing her internal organs. Her anatomical heart was black as pitch. Her fingers with the skin peeled back were claws.

Did Joey see her this way? Did he loathe her?

Her stomach wrenched in a painful spasm. She'd lost her last friend. Bile churned at the back of her throat, and she raced to the bathroom where she vomited into the toilet bowl. She flushed. And vomited again.

It was frigid in here. Weakly she pulled aside the shower curtain. The window was broken. This must have been how the intruder got inside. He broke the glass and climbed through the window while Joey was too absorbed in his artwork to notice the noise. Poor Joey! Joey who thought her heart was a cinder of hard black anthracite.

Still clutching her knife, Nicole slumped to the floor and leaned against the porcelain bathtub. Which was how Sheriff Mace Sheridan found her. She recognized him from the café, where he often had lunch and always left a generous tip.

Pistol drawn, he looked down at her. In his black Stetson and shearling coat, he completely filled the bathroom doorway. "Nicole?"

"There's blood in the studio."

He focused on the weapon in her hand. "What happened?"

Helplessly, she said, "I don't know."

"Are you injured?"

Only in her heart. Her cold black heart. "I'm not hurt."

"That's good," he said. "Now, I want you to give me that knife."

What did he think she was going to do? Lunge at him? She barely had the strength to hold the knife handle toward him.

He tossed the blade into the hallway and holstered his gun. "You stay in the bathroom while I take a look around."

She nodded. The chill sank deeper into her flesh, into her bones. She ought to get to her feet, change clothes and face the situation. But these simple acts seemed overwhelming. Shivering, she closed her eyes.

Somehow, she had to find the strength to face a police investigation. She'd been here before. Arrested twice before she was eighteen. Questions from cops made her nervous, even when she'd done nothing wrong. She hated confrontations that made her feel flustered, frightened and furious. The three *Fs*. She could also add a fourth: failure. An accurate assessment of her life after twenty-six years.

Oh, hell, this shouldn't be happening. She'd thought she was safe in Elkhorn, but everything was falling apart. Her carefully constructed sanctuary was being dismantled, brick by brick.

"Nicole."

At the sound of her name, she startled as if waking from an endless nightmare and stared up at the sheriff. "Are you already done?"

"I need to take care of you before I do anything else," he said. "Are you strong enough to stand up?"

"Maybe."

He held out his hand toward her. Dumbly, she stared at the very masculine appendage, all muscle and tendon. She raised her gaze to his face. His high cheekbones, dark brown eyes and well-tanned complexion hinted at Native American heritage. One of the waitresses at the café had mentioned that the sheriff was part Ute. Nicole noticed the gleam of a silver necklace at his throat.

"Come on," he urged. "Take my hand."

Though she'd seen him dozens of times before, this was the first time she realized that he was a very good-looking man. If she'd had any vestige of self-respect, she would've pulled herself together so he wouldn't think badly of her. But she had no pride left.

She placed her hand in his, and he pulled her upright. He calmly reassured her, "You're going to be okay."

How would he know? She tried to maintain her balance, but her knees were weak. She slumped against him. "I can't move."

"It's okay." He patted her shoulder. "Take all the time you need."

His kindness stirred the lonely emptiness inside her. A tear spilled down her cheek, and she buried her face against the sheriff's coat rather than show him this sign of weakness.

He didn't shove her away. Instead, he sat on the toilet seat and cradled her against his chest. His body heat warmed her. The circle of his arms protected her. His closeness felt soothing, and she trembled as a shred of the pain that enshrouded her heart unraveled. It would be so good to have someone to lean on, someone she could trust.

That was a luxury she never owned. Not even when she lived with Derek and had all the money in the world. *Derek!* She couldn't let him find her. Her survival depended upon keeping her true identity a secret. She mustn't let down her guard. Not even with a sheriff. *Especially* not with a sheriff.

Her spine stiffened, and she pushed away from him. "I'm better now, Sheriff."

"You can call me Mace."

"Okay, Mace." With an effort she pulled herself together. "I'm worried about my roommate. Joey Wentworth. He's not here."

Mace's dark eyes studied her. "That's his Beemer parked out front."

"How do you know it's not mine?" she asked.

"Because you drive a Ford Escort. I saw it pulled off to the side of the road on my way over here."

The sheriff had been watching her. He knew what kind of car she drove. Nicole couldn't let him know too much; such knowledge could only hurt her. Fear surged inside her, giving her the strength to stand on her rubbery legs. She braced herself against the tile of the bathroom wall. "I'm cold."

"It's freezing in here. Let's go to your room."

When he took her arm to guide her out of the bathroom, she recoiled. "I can make it by myself."

"Fine with me." He gestured toward the hallway. "You need to change out of those wet clothes and get warmed up. You might be in shock."

"I don't think so." She staggered into the hall and aimed toward her bedroom. "When I was eleven, I broke my ankle and went into shock. I memorized what it felt like."

If she'd been in shock, she'd be detached from all pain, floating disembodied on a fluffy cloud. Right now, she was sharply aware of the chill and the empty ache in her belly.

"Broke your ankle," Mace said in a friendly, conversational tone. "Skiing accident?"

"No." She'd been pushed down a flight of stairs by her stepfather. It was an incident she didn't intend to share. "I'm not in shock. I'm hungry and tired."

In her bedroom, she intended to go directly to her closet and find other clothes, but her emotional and physical exhaustion dragged her down. With a moan, she sprawled on her back across her torn-apart bed.

The dampness from her parka soaked into the crumpled comforter, but she didn't care. She'd have to clean all the bedding, anyway.

"Listen, Nicole. I haven't worked up this crime scene. So I'd appreciate if you change out of your clothes and don't touch anything else. Do you understand?"

"Yes." But she didn't move.

"If you're not well, I can call an ambulance."

"I'm fine." She didn't want to deal with all the questions asked in a hospital. She forced herself to sit up. "Let's get started with the investigating. Do you have questions for me?"

"Yeah," he said. "Who did this?"

Derek. His name flashed across her brain like a neon sign. But she couldn't tell the sheriff about her suspicion. If Derek thought she'd mentioned him to the police, he'd find a way to make her suffer.

She cleared her throat. "I have no idea who might have done this. A robber. Don't you think so?"

"Tell me what happened after you left work tonight."

"I ran out of gas. I thought I had half a tank, but Joey borrowed my car and didn't fill it up. I was stranded on the road, and it was all his fault. I was so mad I could have—" She stopped herself before saying she could have killed her roommate. Given that Joey was missing, it wasn't wise to mention her homicidal thoughts.

"You could have done what?" Mace prompted.

"Given him a piece of my mind," she said. "But I didn't have the chance. When I got to the cabin, the front door was unlocked. I came inside and found this mess. I went to the kitchen and called 9-1-1."

"Is that when you grabbed the knife?"

She nodded. "I thought Joey might be hurt, and I went looking for him. When I saw the blood on the floor in his studio, it was…horrible. I got sick in the bathroom. Then you came."

"What made you think Joey was hurt?"

"There was violence here," she said. "The cabin is torn to pieces."

"Anything missing?"

"All my money." She pointed to the cigar box. "I kept my cash in there, hidden in the bottom of my hamper. Every time I get a hundred dollars in crumpled-up ones, I exchange it for a fresh new hundred-dollar bill."

"How much?" he asked.

"Nearly two thousand dollars."

He picked up the cigar box by the edge. Then he placed it in a plastic bag he took from his pocket. "Anybody handle this box besides you?"

"Nobody knew about my money."

"We might be able to get fingerprints," he said. "Anything else missing?"

"My jewelry box was emptied. It's no great loss. There's nothing I can't replace for a couple of bucks at the Wal-Mart."

"What about Joey? Does he keep anything of value at the cabin?"

"I don't really know." she said. "His studio is his private space and I never go in there unless I'm invited. That doesn't happen unless Joey is using me as a model."

"He's an artist?"

"And very talented," she said with more loyalty

than accuracy. Joey was competent, but he was no Rembrandt.

"Does he sell his artwork?"

"Joey's paintings hang in some of the most prestigious offices in Denver." That much was true. Joey had told her that his uncle Blake, CEO of Wentworth Oil Exploration, had purchased several pictures.

Mace removed his Stetson and ran his fingers through his thick, shiny black hair. It was almost as if he was scratching his head, puzzling out answers to questions he hadn't yet asked. "As far as you can tell," he said, "nothing important was stolen. Except for your cash money."

"That's right."

"I'll leave you here to change out of those wet clothes while I get started on the forensics."

"Doing what?"

"Looking for evidence. You know, dusting for fingerprints." Mace headed toward the bedroom door, then he paused and turned back toward her. "By the way, how were you and your boyfriend getting along?"

"Joey isn't my boyfriend. We're roommates."

"Any arguments recently?"

She frowned. Why was he asking her about her relationship with Joey? "We get along fine. No problems."

His dark eyes regarded her steadily. She saw resolute stubbornness in the set of his chiseled jaw. Without speaking a word, his expression told her of his determination. He would discover all her secrets. Therefore, Mace was dangerous.

Nicole had to escape from Elkhorn. As soon as she knew Joey was safe, she'd be gone.

Chapter Two

Outside the cabin, Mace walked along the edge of the muddy driveway to avoid scuffing up tire tracks that might be evidence. Though it was his professional duty to collect the forensic data and treat this crime scene seriously, he considered the supposed robbery at the Wentworth cabin to be little more than a prank.

The way he figured, these two roommates had an argument, then Joey tore the cabin apart to teach Nicole a lesson. Unfortunately, he went one step too far by stealing her savings. The little weasel would have to be tracked down in order to get her money back.

Not that Mace considered Nicole to be a blameless victim. He knew she was lying to him. He could see it and feel it. This pretty woman had something to hide.

At his white Ford Explorer with the sheriff logo on the door, Mace gathered his evidence kits and a camera to record the crime scene. He called Barry at dispatch on his cell phone.

"I'm at the Wentworth cabin," Mace said.

"Everything okay?"

"An apparent robbery. No serious injuries." He'd give Barry the details later. "Put out an APB on Joey

Wentworth. He's disappeared and left his 2002 BMW behind.''

''Whoa, it's a crime and a half to abandon that mighty fine vehicle.'' Barry chuckled. ''How's Nicole taking this?''

''Not great,'' Mace said.

''She's a cute little thing. Not too friendly, though.''

A cute little liar. ''Barry, I need you to pull up Joey Wentworth's record on the computer.''

''Sure enough. And I'll check his prints with the FBI, maybe run his ID through the NCIC.''

''I don't think we need to go into the National Crime Information Center just yet,'' Mace drawled. ''Joey's gone missing. That doesn't mean he's planning to start a crime wave in Elkhorn.''

''I'll have the basic data in a sec.''

Barry's voice sounded way too cheerful for near midnight on a Monday night, but the dispatcher was a night owl. His work preference was from ten o'clock at night to dawn, alone at the sheriff's offices at the county courthouse except for his radio, which was always tuned to a country-western station. During those quiet hours, Barry transformed the stacks of half-baked reports from the other deputies into coherent directives for the following day. He was the brain behind the brawn.

Mace's first act after being elected sheriff three years ago was to hire Barry away from the Denver PD where they'd been partners. Barry wasn't the greatest detective in the world, wasn't much of a marksman, and had a sweet tooth that kept him from being in top physical condition. He was, however, sharper than a double-edged razor when it came to computers. He'd taught their previously antiquated system to sort, file, record, sing, dance and whistle "Dixie."

"No outstanding warrants," Barry said. "I'm looking at Joey's record on the computer. Nothing but a couple of speeding tickets. From the photo on his driver's license, I'd say he's kind of a wuss."

"He does oil paintings. Nicole says he's pretty good."

"A young guy who claims to be an artist and drives a brand-new Beemer," Barry summarized. "I'm smelling a spoiled rich kid."

"Thanks, Barry. I'll finish my investigation and drop off the paperwork later."

"Later," Barry echoed.

Back in the cabin, Mace slipped on a pair of disposable latex gloves so he wouldn't contaminate the scene with his own fingerprints. If he'd been following correct procedure, he would have gloved up when he walked in the door and he sure as hell wouldn't have allowed Nicole to go back into her bedroom and get dressed. He figured these investigative lapses were no big deal. More than likely, Joey would call and this whole mess would probably be cleared up before dawn.

Using a digital camera, Mace took photos of Nicole's muddy footprints on the kitchen floor. Though not quite sure what he was looking for, he rifled through the drawers, checked in cabinets and took a look in the trash can. Nothing seemed unusual. After he photographed the locked and dead-bolted back door, there wasn't much else to investigate in the kitchen. It looked clean.

So did Nicole when she joined him in the kitchen.

She'd changed into jeans and a dark-blue sweater that brought out the blue in her wide-set eyes. Barry had called her cute, but Mace wouldn't use that description. Cuteness implied a soft, fuzzy bunny rabbit. Nicole Ferris looked angular, like a tawny cougar who scraped a living from the arid foothills of the high Colorado desert.

He didn't know exactly what to think of her. When he first entered the cabin and saw her with the knife in her hand, he thought she might be capable of murder. Then she collapsed in his arms and clung to him with a desperation that went far beyond the usual fear and anger of a robbery victim. A strange, wordless communication had passed between them. Somehow it gratified him to be there for her when she needed comfort.

"I'm making coffee and a sandwich," she said curtly. "If you want something, you have to serve yourself. I don't bring my work home with me."

"Do whatever you want in the kitchen," Mace said, "I'm done collecting evidence in here."

"Did you find any clues?"

In spite of her brisk attitude, he sensed an undercurrent of emotion. "Nicole, I'll be honest with you. I think Joey is behind this robbery."

"You're wrong," she scoffed. "He wouldn't take my money. We're friends."

Mace had seen the gruesome portrait in Joey's studio with Nicole posed as the queen of the ghouls. That didn't look like the work of a friendly amigo.

"Besides," she continued, "Joey's loaded with dough. His family owns Wentworth Oil Exploration, an international company. He wouldn't bother with my petty cash."

"Two thousand dollars." Mace leaned against the kitchen doorframe and folded his arms across his chest. "Doesn't sound like petty cash to me."

"Because you're not rich." She measured grounds into a paper filter. "People like Joey live differently than you and me. He might drop a thou on a cashmere sweater and then wear it to chop wood."

She sounded as if she had some acquaintance with the world of cashmere sweaters, and he wondered about her background. All he knew about Nicole was what he'd observed during the past couple of months she'd worked at the Elkhorn Café. Not chatty, but good at her job. She kept the coffee mugs full. And she was a pleasure to watch—graceful as a dancer. Even when serving up four heavy platters of chicken-fried steak, her movements were smooth and controlled. And tidy. A very neat person, she always braided her long blond hair without a single strand out of place.

Right now her hair was mussed. Delicate tendrils escaped the braid and swirled beside her cheeks. When her hair was free from all restraints, the silky texture must be beautiful as the sunlight on autumn aspens. "Before you moved to Elkhorn, what kind of work did you do?"

"I've always been a waitress."

"In Denver?"

"Denver, San Francisco, Seattle."

"Always in cities." That made sense. Her attitude was way more city than country. "Have you ever done any other kind of work?"

"Not really."

He ventured into her personal life. "Ever been married?"

"Excuse me?" Her attempt at a disdainful glance fell short when the corner of her eye twitched nervously. "What does my marital status have to do with a robbery?"

Maybe a lot. A jealous ex-husband or fiancé might not like the idea that she had a male roommate. Though Mace was fairly sure that Joey had torn the rooms apart, he needed to consider other possibilities. He felt there was something he was missing in this investigation. Something important.

Staring at the coffeemaker, he willed the machine to drip faster. A jolt of caffeine might get his brain working at full speed. "How long have you been living with Joey?"

"I resent your implication that we're living together. We're *roommates*. There's nothing romantic between us. I pay him rent every month, and he lets me stay here." Her full lips pulled into a frown. "Why do you think Joey robbed me?"

"A couple of things," Mace said. "If this was a robbery for profit, the thieves missed a bet by not taking the television and VCR."

"I thought of that," she said. "I'll bet the robbers changed their minds about taking other stuff after they found my money."

"These robbers," he said. "How do you suppose they got inside the cabin?"

"It's obvious! They broke in through the bathroom window."

"Is that what you think?"

"Of course," she snapped.

Though she tried to act snippy, Mace noticed the tension in her forehead and a sheen in her eyes that might be unshed tears. He sensed that she was scared, but that didn't mean he was ready to put up with her sassy attitude.

He met her gaze, unsmiling. He was the one in charge, and she needed to understand that fact. "Pay attention, Nicole. And I'll explain."

"I'm all ears."

"There was no broken glass in the bathtub. The shards were outside on the ground which means the window was broken from the inside."

"So what?"

"Nobody came into the cabin through that window. And there are no footprints on the ground outside. So nobody went out that way, either." He paused, allowing the facts to sink in. "You understand what I'm saying? Your pal, Joey, broke the window to make it look like there were robbers."

She turned away from him, opened the fridge and pulled out a loaf of wheat bread, mustard, a package of baloney and some cheese. Her frugal dinner explained how she'd been able to save a couple thousand dollars while working as a waitress at the Elkhorn Café.

"Here's another thing," Mace continued. "If there were robbers, how do you suppose they managed to come into the cabin and do all this damage without tracking in any mud? It's been snowing and sloppy all day. But the only footprints in here are yours."

Staring at the kitchen floor, she said, "What about the blood in Joey's studio?"

"It's insignificant. I've bled more when I cut myself shaving. And so, taking this evidence into account, I'd say your cabin is a fake crime scene."

"And you think Joey did it?"

"From that gruesome portrait in his studio, I suspect he's ticked off at you. Maybe you two had an argument.''

''We didn't fight,'' she insisted.

She turned back to the fixings for her sandwich, neatly spreading the mustard on bread, then adding baloney and cheese, then another squirt of mustard. Her actions were slow and deliberate as though she needed to concentrate on this nongourmet preparation.

Mace assumed that she was buying time, but he didn't understand why. What was she hiding? Why was she protecting Joey? ''Tell me more about your roommate. In addition to his painting, does he have a job?''

''He spends a lot of time in Denver. Sometimes he takes art classes. I guess that makes him a student.''

''Kind of old to still be in school.''

''Twenty-six,'' she said. ''The same age as I am.''

''How'd you come to be roommates?''

Carefully she lifted her sandwich. With infuriating slowness, she nibbled a dainty bite and dabbed at the corner of her mouth with a paper napkin.

Though she was pretending to be ladylike, her tactics were a good way to avoid questions. She was damned good at putting him off. He wondered if this wasn't the first time Nicole had undergone a police interrogation. Maybe he should have asked Barry to check Nicole's criminal record instead of Joey's.

Matching her supposed calm, he opened a cabinet, took out a mug and helped himself to coffee while the stubborn silence stretched between them. This was a contest to see who could outlast the other. Mace leaned back against the door frame. He could stand here all night. Stamina was his middle name.

She darted a nervous glance in his direction. Then another. Finally she said, "I forgot your question."

He knew she was prevaricating. She hadn't forgotten that he'd asked about how she and Joey became roommates. "I'm on your side, Nicole. I want to help you get your money back."

"Right. That's your job."

"It's my choice," he corrected. "I'm required to collect the evidence, file reports and make a reasonable attempt to find your missing cash."

"Your job," she repeated. "That's what cops do."

"The amount of effort I put into this investigation is my choice," he said. "If this alleged robbery turns out to be a spat between roommates, I'm not inclined to waste much time looking into it."

"But Joey's missing," she said.

"An interesting twist, but easily explained. He could be spending the night with a friend. He could have hitched a ride to Denver."

"Or maybe he's lying in a ditch with his skull cracked open."

"Given the setup, I doubt that." He sipped his coffee. "Don't make this hard for me. Just answer my questions. How did you meet Joey Wentworth?"

"In Denver," she said. "He mentioned his cabin, and I jumped at the chance to come here."

Mace didn't buy that story. "Far as I know, Elkhorn isn't on anybody's top-ten list of favorite destinations. People are born here. Or they end up here. Not many come to live here on purpose."

"I needed a break. I wanted to come someplace peaceful."

Night shifts at the Elkhorn Café weren't anybody's idea of a relaxing vacation. "Give me a more specific reason. When you first came to Elkhorn, were you and Joey dating?''

"How many times do I have to tell you? We're not lovers, and we never have been."

Mace had a hard time believing that any red-blooded male could live with a woman who looked like Nicole and not form an attachment. "Is Joey gay?"

"Not that I know of." She exhaled a ragged breath. "I'm not trying to be difficult, Mace. But I can't believe Joey took my money and messed up the cabin. It simply doesn't make sense."

"Fine," he said. "Let's come at this from another angle. Is there somebody else who might want to do you harm?"

"No," she said too quickly. The color in her face rose quickly. Her cheeks flushed red. "I can't think of anyone who might want to hurt me."

There was the lie. Mace saw it clear as a thunder-head rising above the mountains. She was scared of someone in her past. "You can tell me," he said.

"Nothing to tell."

The wall phone in the kitchen rang, and her self-control shattered. She dropped her sandwich on the mud-tracked linoleum floor. "Should I answer?"

He nodded. "It's your house."

She grabbed the phone off the hook, glad for the interruption. Mace's questions were coming far too close to the truth.

She cleared her throat. "Hello?"

"Nicole, it's me."

Joey! "Are you all right? Where are you?"

"Kidnapped." His voice was weak. It sounded as if he'd been crying. "I've been kidnapped."

She was shocked. Never in a million years would she have suspected kidnapping. "Who did this?"

"They want $800,000. You've got to call my uncle Blake in Denver. Don't screw this up, Nicole. Please."

"Are you okay?" She remembered the blood on the floor in his studio. "Did they hurt you?"

"It's not too bad."

But she could hear his pain. She imagined his fragile wrists bound together. He wasn't strong enough to stand much abuse. Angrily she said, "Joey, you tell them that they won't get a penny if you're injured."

"I'm not in a position to make demands. Nicole, you're the only one I trust. Do this for me. Do exactly what they say. They're watching you."

A shudder trickled through her. "Are they near the cabin?"

"Eight hundred thousand. Unmarked bills." he said. "Call Uncle Blake and tell him to bring the money to Elkhorn."

The phone went dead.

Waves of emotion crashed over her. Flustered. Frightened. Furious. This was crazy! Though she hadn't believed the sheriff's conclusion that Joey had staged this robbery, that explanation would have been so much better.

When Mace took the telephone from her unresisting fingers, she said, "Joey has been kidnapped."

"Tell me exactly what he said."

"They hurt him." She despised the brutality. Rage boiled up inside her. "How could they? Joey's just a kid. He's—"

"The same age as you are," Mace said. "What are the demands?"

"Eight hundred thousand dollars. I'm supposed to call his uncle in Denver and tell him to bring the money here."

"What else?"

"They're watching me." Disconcerted, she stared at the kitchen window. Were they watching now? Hiding in the trees beyond the lights of the cabin? She imagined the eyes of faceless strangers, probing her life and her secrets.

"They must still be in the area," Mace said. "Did Joey give any indication of where they'd taken him?"

"No."

"I want you to write down every word of your conversation. Every impression. Every sound."

He took a cell phone from his inner pocket and walked into the front room to make his call. From his professional tone, she knew that he was starting the law enforcement gears into motion, summoning his deputies. And the FBI? The Feds were supposed to be called on a kidnapping, weren't they?

In a federal investigation, her real identity would surely be brought to light. All of her known associates and acquaintances would be questioned—including Derek.

Though she took solace in the realization that Derek had nothing to do with the vandalism at the cabin, her relief was short-lived. As soon as he knew she was in Elkhorn, he would come here. He'd force her to come back to him.

She had to escape before it was too late. She'd make the phone call to Joey's uncle, and leave town before the Feds arrived.

She tugged at Mace's sleeve. "My car," she said.

"Can somebody put gas in my car and bring it back here?"

"Tomorrow's soon enough," Mace said. He was still on the phone, issuing orders.

"Please," she said. "I need my car."

Mace completed his call and disconnected. "You're not going anywhere tonight."

"Why not? Am I under arrest?"

She saw suspicion in his dark brown eyes. All of a sudden, he looked like a cop. Cold and hard. And accusing. He asked, "Is there a reason I should arrest you?"

"Of course not. I have nothing to do with Joey's kidnapping."

"Eight hundred thousand dollars." He gave a low whistle. "That's a lot of money. I'm thinking a little taste of that cash might belong to you."

She almost laughed out loud. "No amount of money is worth…"

"Worth what, Nicole?"

Exposure. She couldn't stand to be seen in the glaring light of an investigation. Her life depended on remaining hidden. "I'm not a kidnapper."

"Tell me who you are."

"Nobody. I'm a waitress at the Elkhorn Café."

Her survival instincts took over, and she pushed her fears aside, hiding them behind a thick stone wall. Deep inside she was a frightened, abused child. Her inner self cowered as she waited for the blows to fall.

Outwardly she presented bravado. "I don't have to answer any of your questions. I want a lawyer."

He held out his cell phone. "Call one."

"Wait a minute," she said. "Aren't you supposed to provide a lawyer for me?"

The hint of a smile touched his lips. "That's how it works in the city."

"Are you telling me that it's different in Elkhorn? That you've got some kind of special frontier code of justice?"

"If you want to try calling the county D.A. in the middle of the night, go right ahead. But you're not under arrest," he said.

"Then I can leave," she concluded.

"Sure you can," Mace said. "But the kidnappers are going to call back. And they'll want to talk to you. Even if Joey isn't your boyfriend, do you want to bail out on him?"

She heard a sound out front. Mace's deputies were already arriving. A kidnapping in Elkhorn would be a very big deal. And she was stuck in the middle of it. Trapped. If she fled, Joey might be hurt. She wouldn't abandon him, couldn't be that cruel. "You're right, Mace. I have to help Joey. He trusts me."

Mace nodded. "I'd appreciate if you stay in the kitchen while I check in with my deputies out front."

"What if the phone rings?"

"Don't touch the phone until we've had a chance to trace Joey's call."

When Mace strode from the kitchen, all the energy went with him. She sagged against the counter. The immediate danger wasn't aimed in her direction. This time it was about Joey. Though he could be the most annoying person on earth, he needed her. And she owed him. The first time they'd met was in Denver. At a cemetery.

She'd gone there to place flowers on the grave of her husband's elderly housekeeper, Marlene, who had died of a heart attack. Marlene was a kind woman, and Nicole mourned her passing.

Because her father had died when she was seven and her mother followed when she was fifteen, Nicole took the rituals of mourning very seriously. She placed a bouquet of flowers against the gravestone and patted the fresh sod. "Rest easy, Marlene."

Joey came up behind her. "Your mother?"

"A friend," Nicole said.

She stood and faced him. It was strange for a person to strike up a conversation in a cemetery, and Joey's appearance fitted the role of a very odd duck. He stood only a few inches taller than Nicole, and he was skinny as a wraith with a disheveled mop of dark hair and pale, piercing blue eyes. Crazy eyes. A tight, paint-stained sweater stretched across his scrawny chest, and his plaid trousers looked like something Charlie Chaplin might have worn.

He pointed at a mausoleum on the other side of the winding cemetery road. "I was here visiting my parents. Both dead. Plane crash outside Aspen."

"I'm sorry."

"Six years ago," he said, scuffing his toe on the new sod of Marlene's grave. "I'm still mad at them."

"Why?"

"They screwed around with my inheritance. Didn't think I was responsible enough to handle all that money. It's in a trust fund, and I can't touch the principal until I'm thirty. All I've got is a monthly stipend and a lousy cabin in Elkhorn."

"Where's that?" she asked.

"The middle of nowhere. It's a great little place if you want to hide out from the rest of the world."

Which was exactly what she wanted. Nicole had

stayed in touch with Joey. They'd met for coffee a couple of times. Four months later, when she fled from Derek, she joined her strange new friend in Elkhorn.

Now it was time for her to return the favor. Joey needed her help, and she wouldn't let him down.

Chapter Three

Outside the Wentworth cabin, Mace approached the two deputies—Philips and Greenleaf—who responded to his call for backup. They stood side by side in the headlights of their vehicle, and they were itching for action.

After Mace outlined the situation, Deputy Hank Philips, a skinny kid with shaggy brown hair too long for regulations, could barely contain his excitement. "Damn, Mace. A real kidnapping?"

"It appears so."

The other deputy, Mike Greenleaf, was part Ute, like Mace. He considered himself to be a ladies' man. Nodding toward the cabin, he asked, "Should I look after Nicole?"

"Heck, no," Philips said. "We ought to be collecting evidence. How much money do the kidnappers want?"

"Eight hundred thousand," Mace said.

The two young deputies exchanged glances and poked each other in the ribs. Though Mace knew they were both good men who could be counted on to obey orders and do their jobs, Philips and Greenleaf were basically country boys with more good intentions than experience in crime solving. "Calm down," Mace said.

"Easy for you to say," Philips responded. "You probably handled a million kidnappings when you were a big-city homicide detective in Denver."

"Not hardly."

"Where do we start?" Philips asked. "I've got a fingerprint kit in the trunk."

Further contamination of the crime scene would be unwise. "I want you to stay out here," Mace said. "Keep your eyes open. The kidnappers might still be in the area."

"Yes, sir."

"When Barry gets here, send him inside."

Philips's head bobbed so hard it looked like it might detach from his spindly neck. "You got it, Mace. You're the boss."

The boss? Mace pivoted and stalked back toward the cabin. He sure as hell didn't deserve to be the man in charge. He'd seriously misjudged this crime scene. His handling of evidence was as clumsy as a rookie on his first case. He felt like a fool and had no one to blame but himself.

Damn it! He needed to get a grip. Mace paused in the night. The wet snow no longer sputtered. A strong wind had swept down from the mountains and wiped the clouds from the sky, where a waning moon hovered at the far edge of midnight.

In moonlight, truth was distorted. Nighttime was the purview of the trickster.

As a boy, Mace often visited the Ute reservation at the south edge of Sterling County and listened as his grandfather, Tata Charlie, told the story of Jackrabbit, who disguised his ears as two feathers and gambled with unwary braves, winning easily until he stood too close to the campfire. In the firelight, everyone could see he was only a rabbit. Trapped in a sack, Jackrabbit was eaten for dinner.

The wise man waits with patience until the clever trickster makes a mistake and gets caught. Mace needed to be wise. And patient. Remembering the lessons of Tata Charlie, he resolved to forget his injured pride and seek only the truth.

In the cabin's kitchen, he found Nicole leaning against the counter, nibbling around the edges of another sandwich. She shouldn't be here, wandering around and touching things. Nicole was, at the very least, a witness. At the very worst, a suspect.

"What happens next?" she asked.

"I call the FBI field office in Denver. This becomes their case. Kidnapping means they're in charge."

"You don't look real happy about it," she said.

He frowned. "Why would I be?"

"If the FBI takes over, the kidnapping isn't your problem anymore."

"Everything that happens in this county is my problem."

Her delicate eyebrows arched. "Well, well, Mace. That's a highly developed sense of responsibility you've got there."

"That's the way I am." And he wasn't about to apologize. Not to her. Not to anyone.

"Have you always been so territorial?"

Her teasing grated on his nerves. "I thought you cared about solving this crime."

"I do," she said.

But she still acted the part of the trickster, deflecting direct questions. He needed to look beyond her attitude in order to see the truth. "You don't much like cops."

"You're right. I don't." She finished her sandwich. "But I truly care about what happens to Joey. What should I do to help?"

"You could start by telling the truth," he said.

"I haven't lied to you."

He remembered how nervous she'd been when he'd asked if there was someone who wanted to do her harm. "You didn't become a waitress at the Elkhorn Café because you needed a break from stress. You're hiding from someone. Who's after you?"

Her full lips pressed together in a straight, obstinate line. She'd had enough time to gather her emotional resources and rebuild her emotional barriers which—he realized—were considerable.

Her chin lifted. "Joey's kidnapping has nothing to do with me."

His gaze searched her face. For a moment he was distracted by her innate physical charms. Though she wore no makeup and kept her hair in a plain braid, Nicole was pretty as a movie star. Her forehead, cheekbones and jawline were perfectly proportioned in a heart-shaped face. Her warm beauty made a good disguise for cold, hard lies. "Do you have a criminal record, Nicole?"

"I was arrested twice before I was eighteen," she admitted. "Minor stuff. I was at a party where everybody got arrested for disturbing the peace. Another time, I got picked up for trespassing."

From his experience in the Denver PD, Mace knew the likely cause for a minor to be arrested for trespassing. "You were a runaway."

"I was almost seventeen. Old enough to be on my own."

"Not legally." He wondered what kind of dangerous compromises she'd made to survive. "Tell me what you're hiding. After I call in the FBI, they'll learn all your secrets."

"The Feds don't scare me," she said. "Not as much as you do."

Her blue eyes flickered, and he caught a glimpse of her hidden fear. "Why do I scare you?"

"You're different from most cops. They want to make a collar and rack up another arrest on their record. You're not like that. You're after the truth."

It was the highest compliment she could have given him. Therefore, he was suspicious. "Are you playing me?"

Her full lips curved in a grin. "You'll never know."

"Never is a long time," he said. "But I'm a patient man."

And he would find the truth. Even if it meant trapping her in a sack like a trickster jackrabbit.

He turned away from her. Using his cell phone, Mace made his call to the FBI field office in Denver. After several transfers, he finally got through to the proper person. Special Agent Luke Heflin asked, "What makes you think this is a kidnapping, Sheriff?"

"We have a missing person, Joey Wentworth, and a ransom demand for eight hundred thousand."

"Where was he snatched?"

"His roommate found their cabin ransacked and called 9-1-1." Mace glanced over at Nicole. "I was here when the ransom call came through."

"Did you talk to the kidnappers?"

"No, sir," Mace said. "And we haven't yet notified the person in Denver who's supposed to get the cash and bring it to Elkhorn."

Mace outlined what he thought should be the next logical steps: keep the cabin under guard until an expert forensic team from the FBI could investigate. Have incoming phone calls to the cabin routed to somewhere else where Nicole could answer if the kidnappers called again. "And we should immediately notify the person who is supposed to put together the ransom money."

Nicole stood beside him. "Mace, I need to tell you something. It's important."

He didn't appreciate her interruption. "What?"

"Joey said I should be the one to talk to his uncle. He told me not to screw it up. I have to make the call."

Mace informed Agent Heflin about her concern. The agent said he would hook up a three-way connection with Nicole. "Put her on the line."

As Mace handed over his cell phone, he was keenly aware that he'd already been taken out of the loop. The Feds were in charge.

NICOLE HELD THE cell phone to her ear. Her other arm wrapped tightly below her breasts, her fingers clenched into a fist. Though she'd managed to maintain a calm appearance, she was intensely nervous, sweating. Under her bangs, her forehead was damp. Concern for Joey was foremost in her mind, but talking to his uncle ranked high on the anxiety scale.

Joey's uncle, Blake Wentworth, was the CEO of Wentworth Oil Exploration—a company that Joey acronymed to WOE. Though Nicole had never met Uncle Blake, he was a wealthy man and, therefore, might be acquainted with her former husband in Denver. Contact with Blake Wentworth put her one step closer to Derek on a dangerous path she had no desire to follow.

After the FBI agent spoke to Uncle Blake and informed him that there was an apparent kidnapping, he introduced Nicole.

"I spoke to Joey on the phone," she said.

"Who the hell are you?" he demanded.

"My name is Nicole Ferris." Though her married name was Brewer, she'd never changed her social security number and driver's license. There was no way Blake might connect her to Derek through her name.

"Why did Joey call you?" he asked.

"I'm his roommate. I've been staying at the cabin since springtime, paying him rent."

"He never mentioned you."

Silently, she blessed Joey. She'd asked him not to tell anyone about her, and he'd lived up to that promise.

"Wait," Blake said. "Are you the girl in the paintings? The blonde with the braid?"

Nicole said, "I've posed for Joey."

"I've got one of the canvases," Blake said. "It's the best Joey's ever done. If you look anything like this picture, you're very lovely."

"Thank you." She thought it odd that Uncle Blake hadn't inquired about the well-being of his kidnapped nephew. He seemed almost uninterested in Joey's fate.

"Mr. Wentworth," Special Agent Heflin cut in.

"Nicole has more information regarding the details of your nephew's abduction."

"All right," Blake said irritably. "Tell me the bad news. What's the ransom?"

"Eight hundred thousand dollars." She consulted the notes she'd written about her call from Joey. "In unmarked bills. You're supposed to bring the cash to Elkhorn and wait for further instructions."

"And if I don't?"

How could he even think of not complying? "Joey will be hurt. He might already be injured. I found blood on the floor in his studio."

Blake Wentworth cursed under his breath. "Agent Heflin, what do you advise?"

"Is it possible for you to raise that kind of money?" Heflin asked.

"Yes. Joey's parents are dead, and I'm the executor of their estate. They created a trust for Joey, and it's possible for me to access necessary funds in an emergency. But it won't be easy to withdraw that amount."

"Can you have the money tomorrow?"

"I'll need to talk to my attorney," Blake said. "But I have another thought. My company carries insurance against kidnapping. We might be able to go that route."

"Why do you have insurance against kidnapping?"

"I'm the CEO of Wentworth Oil Exploration. We work in several third-world countries where there's a strong possibility of terrorist activity. I took out the insurance policies to protect my family and key employees, but I'm not sure if Joey is covered."

"It'd be lucky for you if he is," said Agent Heflin.

"I'll look into it."

"In the meantime, I advise following the kidnappers' instructions. Get the money together and plan for a trip to Elkhorn tomorrow."

Blake swore again. He seemed more annoyed than concerned, and Nicole felt herself hardening against this man who ought to care about what happened to his nephew. Blake's cruel attitude reminded Nicole of her own childhood rejections, and she ached in her heart for Joey. Her weird, wealthy roommate shared more in common with her than she'd realized. In a way, Joey was as neglected and abused as she had been when her mother remarried and her stepfather turned her life into a living hell.

While Blake and Agent Heflin made arrangements to meet in Elkhorn, she listened. Her sense of outrage increased. These two men sounded as if they were discussing a business transaction—setting up an itinerary, exchanging phone contacts. They didn't say one word about Joey's terror and the potential danger to him.

"Excuse me," she interrupted. "Do you need any more information from me?"

"Not at present," the agent said. "Put the sheriff back on the line."

When she thrust the cell phone toward Mace, a look passed between them. In contrast to Uncle Blake and the FBI agent, the sheriff's dark eyes shone with empathy. She wished he were handling the investigation. At least Mace gave a damn.

Cell phone in hand, he stood at the kitchen counter, occasionally leaning forward to jot a few words into a small spiral notebook. Utterly absorbed in his conversation, he seemed unaware that she existed, and

Nicole studied him, trying to decide if the sheriff was a threat or a savior.

His thumb hitched in the pocket of his Levi's, and his shearling jacket pulled aside, revealing his long, lean torso. At the collar of his blue work shirt, she saw the gleam of a Ute-designed necklace. Turquoise and black beads separated oblongs of silver. Directly below his Adam's apple was a silver bear totem, a symbol of good fortune.

Her gaze slid down the length of his body. Even in casual clothing, he had dressed with care, almost as if he were wearing his sheriff's uniform. The buttons of his shirt lined up exactly with his silver belt buckle and the seam of his Levi's. His square-toed cowboy boots were muddy on the soles and polished on top. She looked up from the floor, all the way up his long, straight legs.

Nicole realized she was staring at his crotch and glanced away. She couldn't allow herself to be attracted to him. Any thought of sexuality must be quashed immediately. Yet a ripple of anticipation stirred her blood. It had been a long time since she'd felt this way. She'd almost forgotten what it was like to be excited by a good-looking man. Life had taught her that men were her enemies. They were animals. She'd never had a relationship that didn't end in pain.

Yet her eyes were drawn to Mace. To his strong profile. To his dark eyes. His lips enticed her. What would it be like to kiss him? What would he taste like? She wondered if his chest was smooth or hairy.

For goodness' sake, stop! She was no better than Uncle Blake or the FBI agent who concentrated on their own business instead of thinking of Joey. She needed to focus on her roommate and forget about the studly sheriff who tantalized her nascent desires.

A relationship with Mace—sexual or otherwise—was out of the question. She intended to leave Elkhorn as soon as possible. When Joey was safe, she'd be gone. On the run again.

She heard the front door to the cabin open, and she darted into the living room. Barry Thompson shuffled inside. Standing in the middle of her ransacked living room, he set down two metal toolboxes, politely removed his cowboy hat and ran his gloved hand across his bald scalp. In his red-and-black-plaid wool jacket with his jeans tucked into the top of galoshes, he didn't look anything like an official of the sheriff's department.

Through his full beard, Barry offered her a bashful smile. "How you doing, kiddo? Hanging in there?"

"Just barely," she said.

"Don't you worry." He removed his wire-rimmed glasses and wiped away the condensation caused by coming inside from the cold. "If anybody can get this mess straightened out, it's Mace."

She thought so, too. Unfortunately, the FBI seemed to be edging Mace out of the picture. "I think the FBI is taking over."

"Ouch," Barry said. "The sheriff isn't going to like that. Not one iota."

"He's protective about what happens around here. He seems to really care."

"Sometimes he cares too much," Barry said.

"What do you mean?"

"He's never been somebody who puts in his hours and goes home. Me and Mace were partners when we were with the Denver PD, and I never clocked so much overtime in my life. Mace wouldn't give up on a case until he'd tracked down every single lead.''

She was glad to hear of his determination. Having Mace involved boded well for Joey. ''What about the FBI?''

Barry leaned close and spoke in a confidential tone. ''If they're not doing what he thinks is right, he'll find a way around them. You see, Mace understands the difference between law enforcement and true justice. A good cop follows regulations and fills in the blanks. A lawman tries to do what's right no matter what the rules advise.''

She liked his philosophical description. ''Are you saying that Mace is willing to break the law?''

''You didn't hear that from me, missy.'' Barry went down on one knee and opened his toolbox. Inside was a lot of interesting-looking equipment. ''One time I saw him bend the regulations to rescue a kid from abusive parents. Another time he released a woman who shoplifted groceries, and hooked her up with the right people at social services.''

Mace sounded too good to be true. If Nicole had run into a cop like him when she was growing up, her calamitous life might have turned out differently.

Barry continued, ''It wasn't until he moved back to Elkhorn and got himself elected sheriff that he could really put his brand of compassionate justice into effect.''

Compassionate justice. What a lovely concept!

Mace ended his phone call and came toward them. Though he seemed utterly in control, a muscle in his jaw twitched. The frown lines between his dark eyes deepened to furrows. ''The Feds are arriving tomorrow," he said. "Also Blake Wentworth will be here with the ransom money."

"Flying?" Barry asked.

"That's right," Mace said. "We're not going to do a full forensic workup on this crime scene. But I would like you to sweep for bugs."

"Why?" Nicole asked.

"The kidnappers told you that they were watching. They might be listening, too."

He led Barry into the kitchen and pointed to the wall phone. "The kidnappers called on that phone. Do a trace, get prior phone records and forward calls from this phone to my place."

"*Your* place?" Nicole asked. "But I need to answer the phone if Joey calls again."

"That's right." His gaze rested upon her. "I'm taking you home with me, Nicole."

Going home with Mace was definitely not in her plans. She needed to be free, ready to flee if the investigation got uncomfortable.

Stepping out of the way while Barry fumbled around with his electronic equipment, she said, "I prefer to stay here. This is my home."

"This is a crime scene. You'll have to leave."

"Then I'll stay at a motel." But how would she pay? The only money she had was tips from tonight. Less than sixty bucks. "The sheriff's department should pay for my room since—"

"A motel isn't safe unless you're guarded, and I don't have the manpower to spare. You'll come home with me so I can keep an eye on you."

"Why do you think there's danger?"

"I don't like to take chances," he said. "At my

place you can take a shower, relax and sleep in a comfortable bed.''

His bed? The thought flitted across her mind, and she shook her head to erase the sensual images of Mace lying naked on white sheets. His long torso. His wide shoulders. His black hair… ''No,'' she said. ''It doesn't seem like a good idea.''

''My sister, Jewel, lives with me,'' he said. ''So you don't need to worry about your reputation.''

''Found one!'' Barry said. He held a small metal disc between his thumb and forefinger. ''It's a short-range bugging device.''

A shiver curled down her spine. ''The kidnappers were listening?''

''Oh, yeah.'' Barry seemed very pleased with himself. ''This bug isn't real sophisticated. Most electronics stores carry stuff like this for the amateur spy.''

The idea of being spied on—by amateurs or professionals—disturbed her. The tiny silver disc made the threat of danger more real. ''All right, Mace. I'll come with you.''

''Get your jacket.''

''Can I pack some of my other clothes?''

''Don't touch anything,'' he said. ''My sister is about your size. She'll have something you can wear.''

Nicole went into her ransacked bedroom and picked up her red parka which was still wet from her long walk to the cabin. Quickly she glanced around. It seemed unlikely that she'd ever live here again.

Though Mace had ordered her not to touch anything, she had a few precious belongings that she couldn't bear to leave behind: a ratty wool scarf that her grandmother had knitted; a small leather-bound diary; and a framed wedding photograph of her parents. She kissed the glass on the picture. It pleased her to see them together, happy and young and unaware of their cruel fate. Both mother and father were dead. Too soon, they had joined the angels.

She stuffed the items in her purse and hurried to meet Mace. She'd lost so many important people in her life—everyone she cared about. Silently she prayed Joey would be safe.

Chapter Four

If she hadn't been so worried about Joey, Nicole would have enjoyed her ride in Mace's Explorer, with the sheriff logo on the door and the red and blue flashers mounted on the roof and the police radio tucked under the dashboard. Of course, she'd been in cop cars before...but never in the front seat.

As he drove from the shelter of tall, frost-rimmed pines onto the paved two-lane asphalt, Mace glanced over at her. "How are you holding up?"

"I'm fine." A little nervous, a little anxious to get out of town. "Joey's going to be okay, isn't he?"

"If this kidnapping is motivated purely by money and Blake Wentworth is willing to pay, Joey's odds are good. If there's something else involved, I can't predict."

They drove past her little blue Escort on the shoulder of the road. Only a few hours ago her major problem was running out of gas. "What do you mean when you say that something else might be involved?"

"A personal grudge. Revenge." Inside his handsome shearling jacket, his shoulders shrugged. "I can't get over the weird setup of the crime scene."

"Does it really matter?" she asked.

"I don't like loose ends."

Her entire life was loose ends. She generally tried to run away before somebody tied the unconnected threads into a noose and looped it around her throat.

"It's like this," he said. "If kidnappers came into the house to grab Joey, why ransack the place?"

"They were looking for something," she suggested.

"But we've already determined that there wasn't anything of value, except your money."

He was right. The crime scene didn't make sense. "And why would the kidnappers break the window to make it look like a robbery?"

"Good question," he said.

"Tell me about the bug." She enjoyed the give-and-take of their conversation. It seemed like Mace was interested in her opinions. "You suspected right away that they'd want to listen in to our conversation. Why?"

"That's what I'd do," Mace said. "I'd want to know the strategy of the opposition."

"It gives me the creeps to think these guys were eavesdropping on every word we said."

"Did you expect a sense of honor? Or respect for your privacy?"

"Well, no." Though she'd known some scary people, Nicole was smart enough to keep her distance. From an early age, she'd learned it was best to run away.

"Kidnappers," Mace said, "are scum. No better than terrorists. They hurt innocent people."

She remembered another clue he'd mentioned. "There were no muddy tracks on the floor in the cabin. So the kidnappers didn't break in. Do you think they're somebody Joey knows?''

"There might be a simpler explanation," he said. "Maybe they just came to the door and knocked. Would Joey open up for a stranger?''

"Probably. And he often forgets to lock up. I have to remind him." Nicole obsessively locked and dead-bolted both front and back doors, often checking twice to make sure she fastened the latch. "Joey's a lot more trusting than I am.''

"He's not as street smart," Mace said. "When you were a runaway, I'll bet you picked up some keen survival skills.''

She realized that he was subtly probing again, trying to tease out more information about her past, and the shift in his focus disappointed her. For half a second it had felt as if they were both on the same side, discussing the crime and trying to puzzle out the clues. His nudge toward her personal history reminded her that she might be riding in the front seat of the cop car, but he still regarded her as a suspect. "You don't trust me, do you, Mace?''

He said nothing. His eyes faced forward, concentrating on the moonlit road ahead of them.

Though she'd never been big on sharing her life story, there was enough distance from her teen years that she didn't mind talking about them. She decided to give the sheriff what he wanted. "Street smart is a neat, clean description for the lessons I learned as a runaway.''

"Why did you leave your home?''

"Long story," she said. "My father died in an accident when I was seven, and Mom didn't cope real well. She slid into a debilitating depression, wouldn't eat and couldn't sleep. Every night, I'd sit by her bed and read to her, as though she was the kid and I was the grown-up.''

"What kind of books?'' he asked.

"Everything. The classics and mysteries and romances. Any kind of story that might cheer her up.''

Nicole's memory of that time was bittersweet. In a few precious instances, she and her mother had bonded at the deepest level, sharing the ache of bereavement. Most of the time, however, Nicole felt like she was groping in pitch-dark, struggling to find her real mother inside this unhappy woman. *Flustered. Frightened. Furious.* At least her constant reading had resulted in an excellent vocabulary.

She continued, "We lost almost everything. Then she hooked up with my stepfather. He paid the bills and rescued us financially, but he was a total bastard, and he hated me.''

"Abusive?'' Mace asked.

"He didn't often hit me.'' After he'd pushed her down the stairs and broken her ankle, Social Services kept an eye on him. After that, he made sure her bruises didn't show. "Even though my mother wasn't often in touch with reality, she'd have noticed if he regularly beat me up.''

She remembered his big ugly face, red with rage. He looked like a demon from hell when he snarled at her. "My mother died when I was fifteen. Heart failure. She had a stroke and hung on for about a week. I read to her then, too.''

In Nicole's diary, her mother's last words were recorded. Unable to speak because of the stroke, her mother scribbled notes to her daughter. Nicole wrote the responses.

Mace said, "You ran away from your stepfather."

"Fast as I could. I went through a bad period when I was trying to figure out how to survive on the streets of San Francisco. Then I became a waitress."

"And moved to Denver," he said.

"There were a couple of other cities in between. But I ended up in Denver." And met Derek. She wasn't about to tell that part of her story.

"And then what?" Mace asked.

"I got tired of cities and moved here with Joey. That's all there is to say."

Mace turned away from the road to look at her. In the glow of the dashboard lights, his dark eyes seemed to measure her. Quietly he said, "You don't trust me, either."

A very perceptive man. Every time she sidestepped a question, he noticed.

The cell phone in his jacket pocket trilled, and he pulled it out to answer. As he went through a series of terse yes-and-no responses, she observed their route. Before they got to the two-stoplight center of Elkhorn, Mace turned toward the mountains. This was an attractive area with a lot of open acreage for farms and ranches.

He disconnected the call and informed her, "Barry traced the phone call from Joey to a cell phone registered to a man who passed away six months ago."

Mace was beginning to think these kidnappers were professional criminals. They were clever enough to use an untrackable cell phone and plant a listening device at the cabin.

He was eager to match wits with them, to outsmart them at their own game. But he wouldn't have the chance. Tomorrow the FBI would be here, and Mace would be relegated to the position of observer.

Nicole asked, "Can Barry determine where the cell phone is?"

"Not unless it's turned on. Then he can triangulate the signal and come up with an approximate location. If Joey calls again, keep him on the phone as long as possible."

"How am I going to be able to take his call?" she asked.

"Barry has the cabin phone number patched through to the private line at my house. The phone will also ring at the sheriff's office, and your conversation will be recorded."

"Wow," she said. "Barry's good at this stuff."

"He's a talented guy," Mace agreed. Barry's skills were wasted in Denver where politics were part of the promotion game. An introvert like Barry usually got overlooked.

"Is he dating anybody?" she asked.

"Don't start," Mace warned. Three years ago, when Barry first moved to Elkhorn, Mace's sister had fixed him up on a disastrous series of blind dates. "Barry can find his own girlfriend. He's a grown-up."

"Even a grown man needs a little shove now and then."

"Maybe he's happy living by himself, doing his own thing."

She scoffed. "He just *thinks* he's happy."

Mace exhaled a resigned sigh. "It's the nature of women to be matchmakers. Always has been. Every spring, the Ute tribes perform a Bear Dance that starts with the women choosing their partners. Though the men pretend to ignore them, they're caught. No matter how hard they try to escape, each brave ends up with the squaw who picked him.''

"A very sensible ritual," Nicole said.

He gave a short laugh. "All of us men might as well accept the fact that we're helpless against your female wiles."

"Have you ever been married, Mace?"

"Once. It didn't work out. I'm told that cops make lousy husbands.''

Though it might be considered unprofessional for him to discuss his personal life with a possible suspect, Mace was too tired to worry about indiscretion. His instincts told him that he'd made the right decision in bringing her to his home. If she was a witness who might be in danger, he'd be there to protect her. If she was involved in the crime, he could watch to see if she made contact with the kidnappers.

"About this phone that's patched through from the cabin," she said. "What if Joey calls right now?"

"Then, you'll be able to answer," he said as he turned at the mailbox and drove down a paved driveway to the ranch house that his father had built.

IT WAS WELL AFTER two o'clock in the morning, not the appropriate time for a tour of the Sheridan ranch house, but Nicole liked what she saw as Mace escorted her through the kitchen and the southwestern-style living room to a long white-walled hall lined with photographs of horses. He opened the second door from the end and stepped inside a simple but charming bedroom, decorated in pastel greens. "You'll sleep here. There's an attached bathroom with toothpaste and shampoo and stuff. Help your-self."

"Thank you," she said. "This is very nice."

"Right here on the nightstand is the phone," he said. "I really don't expect the kidnappers to contact us tonight, but if they call, this phone will ring."

"What should I do?"

"Answer it. Keep them on the line."

She hoped he was right about no calls tonight. The intensity of the day had begun to wear on her. She felt tired and weak. Yet, at the same time, there was a spark that flickered dimly within her like the pilot light on a stove. Though she couldn't quite identify the source of this unusual warmth, it gave her the strength to go on.

Mace opened the top drawer of a cherry wood bu-reau. "There are T-shirts in here. You can use one for sleeping. And you'll find a bathrobe in the closet."

"You're better equipped than most five-star ho-tels."

"We have a lot of visitors in the summer," he explained. "We raise horses, and my sister hosts a couple of riding camps."

"Sounds like fun," she said without much enthu-siasm. Nicole was a city girl who spent more time in taxis than on horseback.

Mace strode toward the door. "My bedroom is next door. If you need anything, holler."

"Mace!"

He turned back toward her, his eyebrows lifted. "What is it?"

"Thank you for everything."

A smile curved his full lips, transforming his appearance from merely good-looking to amazingly handsome. "Sleep well," he said.

He left the room, and she exhaled a breath she hadn't been aware of holding. Now she understood the tiny spark that glowed in the center of her heart. Being around Mace was the cause for this quickening heat. He made her breath come a little faster and caused her muscles to tense—not an unpleasant sensation.

Though she'd be leaving Elkhorn soon, she recorded these feelings in her sensory memory. She wanted to cherish these moments with Mace, to remember every detail so she could replay them after she'd run away to another place where no one cared about her comfort or safety.

Her gaze flitted around the room, too exhausted to fully appreciate the Navajo rug on the hardwood floor and the flowered curtains and the puffy green comforter on the double bed. First, she needed sleep.

She tore off her clothes, slipped into a T-shirt from the bureau, then turned off the overhead light and dived under the covers. The smooth cotton sheets smelled fresh and clean.

As she laid her head on the pillow, she heard a crinkling and felt a sheet of paper. She turned on the bedside lamp. It was a note, written in pen on lined yellow paper. It read: "Meet me at 3:00 a.m. Five fenceposts to the west of the mailbox. Don't tell Mace. If he finds out, I'm dead. Joey."

Her heart constricted. *They were watching.* Were they listening, too? Her hand clapped over her mouth, suppressing the urge to scream or to burst into tears. If there was a bug in this room, she didn't want *them* to hear. How had anyone gotten in here to leave a note? This was the sheriff's ranch. How could the kidnappers dare to deliver this message?

She wanted to call out to Mace, to hand him this scrap of yellow paper and let him deal with the consequences. But *they* might overhear. And *they* would kill Joey if she didn't do as they ordered.

She checked her wristwatch. It was 2:33 a.m. If she was going to meet the kidnappers' demand, she had to move fast.

Her fists clenched and she punched the pillows as hard as she could. This wasn't fair! She wanted to stay on the right side of the law—Mace's side. Yet, she dared not disobey the instructions in the note. Joey's life depended upon her actions.

She needed to be smart. Somehow, she had to find a way out of the house without Mace noticing that she had gone. How could she retrace her path through the darkened house without tripping over something? What if the doors were locked with dead bolts? She paced quickly back and forth. The window! She'd have to go out through her bedroom window!

She yanked aside the curtains, aware that the kidnappers might be watching her right now. Unfastening the latch, she pushed the lower half of the window up. The resulting space was wide enough to slip through.

The door to her room burst open, and Mace stood there, gun in hand. He'd been getting ready for bed, stripped to the waist. The glow from her bedside lamp cast a golden sheen across his smooth, bronzed chest and lean torso.

Her poor battered heart yearned toward him. She didn't want to betray him. She wanted to repay his kindness. She desperately wanted Mace to trust her.

His expression was stern, his lips unsmiling. "What's going on?"

She shoved the note under the edge of the comforter. "I l-l-like to sleep with the window open."

He lowered his gun. In his dark eyes, she saw a glimmer of suspicion. "It's cold tonight. Are you sure you want the window open?"

Deliberately, she lied. "I like the fresh air."

He stood, staring at her. It was obvious that he didn't believe her, but Nicole knew better than to prattle on when confronted. *Stick to one story. Don't add unneeded details.* Joey's survival depended on her ability to convince Mace that all she wanted was a little night air.

Ignoring her rising sense of panic, she tucked her legs under the comforter and forced her lips into a teasing grin. "I like your shirtless uniform. Do you wear your gun when you sleep?"

"Don't con me, Nicole."

"I'm being completely honest about your uniform." Truthfully, she admired his body. "I'm sure other women have told you the same thing."

His shoulders straightened, and the shifting of his muscles enticed her. His skin was the most incredible burnished sienna—the color of the earth itself. Though she'd meant for her smart-aleck compliment to distract him, it was having the opposite effect. She couldn't take her eyes off his body. She wanted to touch him and have him hold her. She wanted to feel his hands upon her flesh. She felt a stirring in the pit of her stomach. Beneath her nightshirt, her nipples tightened.

"Good night," Mace growled.

When the door closed behind him, she collapsed backward on the pillows. *Unbelievable!* After Derek, she never thought she'd be interested in sex again. But Mace turned her on. He made her think that something wonderful might happen if they made love. Unfortunately, she would never have the chance to know what a relationship with Mace might be. She couldn't stay in Elkhorn.

She checked her watch. Only fifteen minutes to make it to the mailbox and meet Joey. There was no more time to think. She darted into the bathroom and turned on the water in the shower to cover the sounds of getting dressed.

Eight minutes until three o'clock. She turned off the tap in the bathroom and made shuffling noises, bouncing on the bedsprings. Then she turned off the light and went to the window. Quickly she slid through the narrow opening.

Outside she crouched on the ground. Waiting, listening. Would Mace charge into her room? Would he catch her trying to escape? She almost wished he would. If she were physically restrained, she couldn't fulfill the kidnapper's demand.

She heard the rustling of wind through tree branches. The night was alive. From the stables near the house, the horses nickered and snorted. In the distance a dog barked. Nicole shuddered. She'd feel far more comfortable with the background noise of city traffic and police sirens to cover her clandestine and probably foolhardy behavior.

Quickly she crept along the edge of the house. At the driveway she checked the time again. Only minutes were left. She ran down the long paved driveway to the road. Out of breath, she reached the mailbox. What had the note said? Five fenceposts to the left? Or the right?

Staring to the right side, she saw nothing. To the left, there was a clump of pine trees. That must be where Joey would meet her. She raced toward the spot. Then she saw him.

"Stay back," Joey warned. "They'll shoot me if you get too close."

He looked ghastly in the moonlight. All color had drained from his face. His hands were tied together. The other end of the rope was lashed to the fencepost.

She took a step toward him.

"Don't come near me," he said. "They're listening. I'm wearing a bug."

"They can't kill you," she said, taking another step. She wanted to yank the ropes free, to run with him to the safety of the ranch house. "They won't get their ransom money if you're dead."

"Listen to me, Nicole. They have long-range rifles. Night scopes. They could shoot me in the leg or in the arm."

Which meant they could shoot her, too. She froze, not daring to look around and try to see the hidden assailants who fixed their sights on her. Standing at the edge of the road in the moonlight, she was an easy target. She couldn't hide.

An involuntary cringe shook her body. Her knees felt weak. Fear replaced her determination to rescue him. She was unable to free him or to save herself. Helpless and hopeless, she remembered her demon stepfather and Derek, looming over her, punishing her without reason. Every faded bruise throbbed with the persistent memory of pain.

"Nicole," Joey said, "I'm supposed to tell you something."

Paralyzed, she could barely speak. "Tell me."

"You can't run away. I know you want to. I know that's what you do. But you can't. You have to stay."

"Why?"

"They want you to deliver the ransom," he said. "They know you're not a cop. They trust you to do what they say."

How could she? Deliver a ransom? Follow instructions? Standing here under the threat of danger, she couldn't even move. "I can't."

"You have to," he pleaded. "You have to be brave. For me."

But she wasn't heroic. She didn't have the strength, didn't have the resources. "I'm sorry, Joey."

"You don't have a choice," he said. In contrast to her abject terror, he seemed controlled. She never expected Joey to have such fortitude. "If you don't do what they say, they'll kill you."

That was why they summoned her here. To deliver a threat.

"Please, Nicole. Say you understand."

"I do," she said.

"Promise me you won't run."

Every instinct told her to flee. Now. To take off on foot if necessary.

"Nicole, they're watching you. They hear every word you say."

Her gaze darted wildly. Danger was everywhere. She was utterly vulnerable. "I won't run away," she said. "I promise."

"Good." His thin, pale face seemed to relax. He

held up his bound hands in an attitude of prayer. "I knew you wouldn't let me down."

"Oh, Joey." A 'sob wrenched from her. "I'm so sorry you have to go through this."

"I'll make it." He nodded toward the ranch house. "Go back inside before Mace notices you're gone."

She wanted to hug him, to cling to him. They were two helpless victims, caught in a maelstrom of hostility. "I won't let you down."

"Go," he said.

She turned back toward the house. Her legs felt leaden. Her gait was clumsy. It seemed like an impossibly long distance back to the house. Logic told her that the kidnappers wouldn't shoot her now. She'd promised to do as they said. Still, she felt their eyes upon her. Their threat had permeated all the way to the marrow of her bones.

At the mailbox, she turned and walked slowly, measuring each step as if she were mounting the gallows. Death and danger were everywhere. To survive, she had to be brave. And she didn't know if that was possible.

At the window to her bedroom, she hoisted herself up with her last shred of strength. Slipping off her shoes and parka, she crawled under the covers, fully dressed, and closed her eyes. Fear coursed through her body. *They* were watching. *They* were listening. And she had to obey or die.

Chapter Five

Crouched behind the tangled, leafless branches of a chokecherry bush near the three-rail whitewashed fence at the end of his long driveway, Mace watched and waited, motionless as a shadow in the moonlit night. The gleam of his .38 caliber automatic pistol was hidden inside the dark sweatshirt he'd thrown on when he realized Nicole had gone out her window.

He'd followed her quickly, noiselessly. In the cleared land at the front of his house, there wasn't enough cover for him to get close to the pine trees beyond the mailbox. From this distance, he'd only been able to overhear a few snatches of Nicole's conversation with the kidnapped Joey Wentworth—enough to know that Joey was wearing a bug and that long-range rifles were trained upon him. Mace had strained his ears. It seemed that Joey wanted Nicole to do something for him. She was afraid, and she'd spoken too softly for Mace to understand her words.

When she stumbled up the driveway to the house, he had stayed put. Later, he'd talk to her. Right now, he needed to track the kidnappers.

Alone at the fencepost, Joey muttered an incoherent phrase. He shifted his weight from foot to foot. Mace noticed that he was wearing sturdy hiking boots. Apparently, the kidnappers had given him enough time to dress before abducting him.

Two men—dressed all in black including black ski masks—appeared from the opposite side of the road. One wore a cowboy hat on top of his ski mask. Talk about dumb! Both carried rifles with night scopes.

"About time," Joey snapped. "I'm freezing."

"Shut up! You want the sheriff to hear?"

"Why didn't you bring the car?" Joey whined.

Mace knew the reason. This road was seldom traveled at night. The kidnappers were smart enough to know that if a car cruised by, he might notice the sound and become suspicious. At the same time, they were stupid enough to lure Nicole out here. Were these guys pros? Or idiots?

With a few yanks on the knots, the one in the cowboy hat untied Joey's wrists and reeled in the length of rope like a lariat.

Together the three men walked down the center of the deserted two-lane road, heading west. Restraining Joey didn't seem to be much of a concern, probably because he had no real chance for escape. Both of the kidnappers were husky men who could overpower the wraithlike Joey without breaking a sweat.

As they walked, Mace crept behind them. In his moccasin slippers, his footfalls were nearly silent. If he'd had time to grab his own long-range rifle with night scope, he might have picked off the kidnappers and rescued Joey. His handgun wasn't accurate enough to risk a showdown with two well-armed men.

At the stand of pine trees, he vaulted over the top

rail of the fence separating his property from the road. Running in a low crouch, he followed his prey.

The three men paused. They stood like statues. The cowboy lifted his head as if scenting the air. He said, "I heard something."

When they turned to peer through the night, Mace flattened his body into a shallow ditch at the edge of the road. Shadows beside a frosted ridge covered him. The icy cold absorbed into his sweatshirt and froze against his cheeks and throat. He held his breath.

Joey said, "I don't see anything."

The scraping sound of their footsteps resumed.

Carefully, Mace rose from the shadows. To avoid being seen, he must use all his wiles, lessons not taught in the police academy where he graduated at the head of his class. Instead Mace remembered his childhood hunting trips with Tata Charlie on the rez. With bow and arrow, they stalked rabbit and elk. Tonight Mace hunted a more dangerous quarry.

If the kidnappers spotted him, they would shoot. He would die. Joey would not be rescued. And Nicole? He didn't know what to think of her. Though her fear seemed real, she had sneaked away from the house without telling him.

When one of the kidnappers glanced over his shoulder, Mace dodged again, hiding behind the trunk of a conifer that separated his property from his neighbor's.

If Nicole had told him that the kidnappers were near, he would have arranged for backup. One of his deputies could have followed the kidnappers in a car. They could have ended this crime before the FBI and Blake Wentworth got involved.

Too late for that now.

On the far side of a crossroad, red taillights flashed once and went dark as the three men approached. In the moonlight, Mace identified the silhouette of a Jeep Wagoneer, a very old off-road vehicle. The Wagoneer hadn't even been manufactured for the past ten or twelve years. The color was black or dark blue. Mace needed to get closer to read the license plate.

As Joey and the two kidnappers climbed inside the vehicle, he positioned himself behind a row of mailboxes. The motor of the Jeep started. The taillights flashed. He saw New Mexico plates and memorized the numbers before they drove away.

Mace stood erect, staring at the empty road. From a distance, he heard the lonely howl of a coyote. A punishing chill sank through his flesh to his bones, but he smiled triumphantly. Though he had not yet won the game, he'd gained an important lead.

HUDDLED BENEATH THE comforter, Nicole waited for sleep that wouldn't come. Her mind was too troubled. Every time she glided toward unconsciousness, she jerked awake. It wasn't fear that kept her from slumber. After a lifetime of abuse, she'd learned to live with terror and had even found that sleep provided a certain mindless solace. The reason she couldn't rest? Guilt.

She'd made the wrong choice, never should have met with Joey without telling Mace. Though the note on her pillow was threatening, she should have figured out a way around the kidnapper's demands. Even if—as she suspected—her room was bugged, she could have found another place to talk to Mace or even to pull him outside. She should have handled this better. How could she expect him to trust her if she went skulking around behind his back?

So what if Mace didn't trust her? She burrowed under the pillow. His opinion didn't matter. Sure, he'd been kind to her, but it wasn't as if they had a bond. When this kidnapping was over, she'd probably never see him again.

Her eyelids snapped open. There was no reason for her to feel so guilty. Joey told her that the kidnappers would kill her if she didn't do as they said—which meant not telling the sheriff. By keeping her secrets, she was saving herself. Her actions were rational, based on survival.

On the other hand, she needed an ally in this investigation. It wouldn't hurt to have Mace on her side when the Feds arrived tomorrow.

Should she tell him? Or not? Both sides of the question had equal weight.

Through the wall, she could hear him moving around in his room. Her guilty conscience tipped the scales. *Tell him.* She threw off the comforter. Still dressed in jeans and sweater from her meeting with Joey, she tiptoed barefoot into the bathroom and turned on the water to cover the sound of her movements in case the kidnappers were listening. Quietly as possible, she crept into the hallway.

Outside the door to Mace's room, she hesitated. If she knocked or called to him, the kidnappers might hear. But how could she just walk inside? What if he slept in the nude?

She noticed a thread of light at the bottom edge of his bedroom door. He must be awake.

Gathering her nerve, she twisted the knob and pushed the door open. Mace stood in the center of the room. He wore a white T-shirt and sweatpants tied with a drawstring, slung low on his hips. In his hand, he grasped his cell phone. When he saw her, his gaze quickly transformed from surprise to anger.

She placed her index finger across her lips to indicate silence. With the other hand, she beckoned for him to follow her.

He growled, "What the hell—"

"Shhhh." She beckoned again.

He grabbed a plaid flannel shirt from the back of a chair and came after her into the hallway.

In the living room, Mace turned on a lamp. She flinched. Were the kidnappers watching? She whispered, "My room is bugged."

She handed him the note from Joey.

Scowling, he read it quickly and said, "This doesn't say anything about a bug."

"I found the note in my room. On my pillow. Don't you think they'd be smart enough to leave a bug behind?"

"They were in your bedroom." His upper lip curled in disgust. "They were in my house."

"I did what the note said," she whispered. "I went out the window and met with Joey."

"You can speak up now. The kidnappers are long gone." He turned away from her and punched a number into his cell phone. "Barry, send two deputies over here. Not Philips and Greenleaf. They need to stay at the Wentworth cabin. And I have a license number for you to trace. New Mexico plates." He rattled off a number. "Call me back on the cell when you have the ID."

"I'm sorry," she said. "I should have told you

right away, but I was afraid for Joey. The note said that if I told you, he'd be hurt."

"They counted on your fear," he said. "Damn it, Nicole, you're smarter than this. If you had told me, I could have—"

"There wasn't time." She was beginning to regret her decision to be truthful. "I only had a few minutes to run out to the mailbox."

"And your instincts told you not to trust me. Right? Never trust a cop." He thrust his arms into the sleeves of his flannel shirt. "You made the wrong decision."

"I said I was sorry."

"You're lucky you aren't dead." His dark brown eyes flared. His jaw tensed. "Those guys had long-range rifles, and you were standing in the moonlight, fully exposed. They could have picked you off easy."

"How do you know that?"

"I followed you," he said.

She should have guessed. Mace was no fool. He'd been suspicious when she opened her window. "My God, if they'd seen you, we'd all be dead."

"But they didn't," he said with a trace of pride. "Tell me what Joey said to you. Don't leave anything out."

"He warned me not to run. He said that if I don't follow their instructions, they'll kill me."

"What instructions?"

"They want me to deliver the ransom," she said. "Because they're sure I'm not a cop."

Mace exhaled slowly as he lowered himself into an armchair beside the fireplace. He stared at her as if he expected something from her. But what?

The silence lengthened and deepened. It grew in

substance until she felt she'd be crushed. Nicole cleared her throat. "Could you please say something."

"I'm thinking."

"Think out loud," she said.

"The kidnappers' behavior was reckless. If you'd told me, I could have called in backup and trapped them. Why take that risk?"

"I don't know. They wanted to scare me, to make sure I'd obey them. Joey made me promise I wouldn't take off before this was over."

"Why does he think you'll run?"

"It wouldn't be the first time." The pattern started when she ran from her stepfather's house. In other relationships in other cities, she'd always fled rather than confronting a bad situation. Right now, she was on the run from Derek. Though Joey didn't know her husband's name, he knew she was hiding from someone who had abused her. "Joey knows me."

"But the kidnappers don't," Mace said.

"Maybe they told Joey that they planned to use me to deliver the ransom and he told them about my…habits."

"You can't run now," Mace said.

His words stoked her ever-present panic. "That's easy for you to say, sitting here in your comfortable house, warm and secure. The only way I know how to survive is to disappear. If I'm invisible, no one can hurt me."

"I won't let that happen," he said. "I promise. I won't let anyone hurt you, Nicole."

Disbelieving, she stared into his face. How could he make good on that promise? Didn't he know that the world was a dangerous place? Life was a fragile proposition. Nobody could guarantee safety.

Yet she knew that Mace meant what he said. He would try—as hard as he could—to protect her.

A glimmer of hope flickered within her, and she cringed, not wanting this faint light to illuminate the very real terror that engulfed her. She'd been on the run all her adult life, fleeing from one disaster to the next. *Life is pain. That's how it works.* And yet… Was it possible that she'd finally stumbled across a man who wouldn't hurt her?

"Believe me," he said.

"I can't." The words wrenched from her throat. "Nobody has ever been on my side."

"Not even your parents?"

"Theirs was the worst betrayal of all. They died."

"I won't die." He grinned wryly. "That's not part of my theory."

She wanted to return his smile, but her face was paralyzed. Fear clenched her tightly in its grip. If she dared to hope, she might be utterly destroyed. "You can't guarantee my safety."

"Let's make a deal, Nicole. You tell me the truth, and I'll make sure nothing bad happens to you. Shake on it."

When he stood and held his hand toward her, she remembered the moment in the cabin when he'd extended his hand and helped her rise from the floor. He was her lifeline, a beacon of safety in a dark, dangerous world.

She clasped his hand, and a strange electricity flowed up her arm. In spite of the hour and her lack of sleep, she felt energized. She took a step closer to him, wanting to feel his arms enfold her again.

A woman's voice echoed from the hallway. "Hello? Mace, what's going on?"

Nicole broke away from him as he introduced his sister, Jewel, and gave her a brief outline of the situation. Jewel listened without comment. She was a handsome woman, slim and tall. Like Mace, she had black hair and dark eyes that reflected intelligence in spite of being awakened in the middle of the night.

"Someone got into the house?" she questioned. "In here? Are you sure?"

"They left a note in the guest bedroom where Nicole was sleeping," Mace said. "Did you remember to lock up?"

"I'm not really sure if I did, but I'll be damned sure to remember after this."

"I've got a couple of deputies coming over," he said. "They'll check all the windows and doors."

"Fine." Jewel tightened the sash on her bathrobe and headed toward the kitchen. "I'd better brew a pot of coffee."

"Don't be too nice to them. I want to get some sleep tonight." Mace turned toward Nicole and took her arm. "You're going to bed. Now."

His concern for her felt good. His touch was even better. She called out toward the kitchen, "Nice to meet you, Jewel. I'm sorry for the disruption."

"Not your fault," she said. "See you in the a.m."

Nicole allowed Mace to lead her down the corridor lined with framed photographs of horses. "Your sister seems nice."

"Don't let appearances deceive you. She's tough as nails. Jewel runs everything around here, including me."

She found it hard to believe that anyone could order Mace around.

When they entered her bedroom, he closed the window and pulled her back into the hall. "Sorry to evict you again, but this is another crime scene."

"And it might be bugged," she whispered.

"I doubt that our kidnappers are using long-range transmitters, but we won't take any chances. I'll have Barry do a sweep through the whole house." He escorted her to his bedroom. "You'll sleep here tonight."

In his bed? "Where will you—"

"Someplace else," he said. "Get some rest. Tomorrow will be a very long day."

He patted her shoulder. For a moment, she thought he might lean close and give her a little kiss on the cheek. Her body involuntarily inclined toward him. A kiss from Mace might not be so bad. It might be marvelous.

"The phone," she remembered. "I need the phone in case Joey calls."

"Good point. I'll bring it in here."

When he left the room, she peeled off her clothes down to her bra and panties. His bed! She would be sleeping in Mace's bed. What sort of dreams would she have?

She slipped between the sheets of the king-size bed and wriggled around, trying to find the spot where Mace usually slept. The pillow still held the imprint of his head, and she rested her cheek exactly in that spot. The bed linen smelled like him—an earthy scent of dried leaves and pine. She imagined him in the bed beside her, protecting her.

There was a rap on the door.

She pulled the comforter up to her chin. "Come in."

Mace entered with the mobile phone in his hand. He placed it on the bedside table beside a digital alarm clock. When he gazed at her, his eyebrow lifted in a sardonic question mark. He seemed to be asking a silent question that had nothing to do with this investigation. It was as though he saw her differently, not like a cop trying to get information from a witness. He was looking at her the way a man looks at a woman. Gently, he said, "Good night, Nicole."

The intimacy in his baritone voice strummed a chord that resonated through her entire body. As she returned his warm gaze, she finally felt relaxed enough to smile. "G'night."

When he turned off the bedside lamp and left the room, she could still feel his presence. Hope burned more brightly within her, like a campfire keeping all the wolves at bay.

As soon as she closed her eyes, she was sound asleep, free from guilt.

THOUGH IT FELT LIKE ONLY a moment before she opened her eyes again, Nicole saw sunlight at the edge of the window curtains. She glanced at the digital clock on the nightstand. It was after eight o'clock.

Though she reveled for a moment in the sensual pleasure of Mace's warm bed, anxiety pricked at her nerve endings. Today, the FBI would arrive. As would Blake Wentworth, Joey's uncle. And the kidnappers expected her to deliver the ransom. She was about to be dumped from the frying pan into the fire.

Quickly, she left the bed, dressed in her clothes from last night and went to the bathroom to wash up.

Her hair was a complete disaster. She unfastened the remnants of her braid, found a brush in the bathroom cabinet and dragged the bristles through the tangles.

Her natural blond hair had always been one of her better features. Thick and wavy, it hung nearly to her waist. She considered leaving her hair loose. Mace might like it that way. Most men did.

She frowned at her face in the mirror. No way should she try to seduce the sheriff. Every time she'd used her feminine wiles, Nicole had gotten into trouble—most notably with Derek. He was a wealthy attorney, a regular at the Denver restaurant where she worked, who never should have given her a second look. Almost as a joke, she'd flirted with him—showing a glimpse of cleavage and sharing hot, sultry glances. Before she knew what was happening, they were married. She became his trophy wife...and his punching bag.

Quickly, she plaited her hair in a tight, neat French braid. Never again would she practice the fine art of seduction. Not with Mace or anyone else.

Before she left his bedroom, she grabbed the mobile phone—a reminder that the kidnappers would call. Sooner or later. And they would tell her how to deliver the ransom. Then, she would leave Elkhorn forever.

In the kitchen, she found Jewel sitting at a long maple table with a ledger open in front of her. October sunlight splashed through windows that were half-covered by blue and white gingham café curtains. "Ready for coffee?" she asked.

"You read my mind," Nicole said. She turned toward the deep blue tiled countertops. "I can get my own."

"You sit," Jewel ordered. "English muffin or homemade banana bread?"

"Bread, please." She placed the mobile phone on the table and sat at the table, hands neatly folded in her lap. "Mace said you run a horse ranch."

"I keep about a dozen head, ranging from champion Arabians to a goofy little burro. I raise them, train them, trade them and sell them." She placed a coffee mug on the table along with a sugar bowl and creamer. "It's a good life."

"Have you always lived here?"

"When I was twelve, I moved to Kentucky to work at a stable with race horses. It was my dream to be a jockey." Standing at the counter, she sliced a thick slab of banana bread. "Then I turned thirteen and grew six inches in a year. If I'd stayed petite like you, I might have ridden in the Derby."

"Funny," Nicole said, adding a dollop of cream to her coffee. "I always wished I could be taller."

"No woman is ever really satisfied with what she's got." Jewel placed the bread in front of Nicole and sat at the table beside her. "And so, to answer your question, I've lived a lot of places besides Elkhorn, but this is home. Three years ago, I came back to stay. My dad needed a lot of nursing after he was diagnosed with Lou Gehrig's disease."

"I'm sorry," Nicole said.

"He passed away a year and a half ago. A shell of the man he once was. It's hard to watch your parents grow old."

Nicole would have given anything to see her parents reach their golden age. "Did Mace move back here at the same time?"

"Just about." Jewel closed the ledger book on the

kitchen table. "At first, I felt guilty about pulling him away from his career as a police detective in Denver. But I think he was ready to leave the big city PD with all its rules and restrictions. As sheriff, he gets to run things his way."

"I've noticed," Nicole said.

Jewel pushed her straight, shiny black hair off her forehead. "He's going to hate having the FBI order him around."

Last night, Nicole remembered, Mace had said Jewel was the one who issued the orders. He'd also characterized his sister as being tough which wasn't Nicole's impression at all. Jewel seemed smart, independent and sensible in a common sense way.

Nicole took a bite of the moist banana bread. "Delicious."

"There's not much left. Last night, the deputies brought their appetites. Mace left a couple of them here to keep an eye on things." She pointed to the mobile phone on the table. "Are you expecting a call?"

"As a matter of fact, I am. From the kidnappers. Barry had the calls from my cabin forwarded to this number."

"Wow," Jewel said. "I still can't believe this is happening in sleepy little Elkhorn."

Nicole took another bite of the tasty bread and another sip of the excellent coffee. She dabbed at the corner of her mouth with her paper napkin.

"You're very ladylike," Jewel said. There was no condemnation in her voice; she was merely stating a fact.

"I'm a neat freak," Nicole admitted. "A place for everything, and everything in its place."

"Is that the way you were brought up?"

"The opposite," Nicole said. "My early life was chaos. Now, I need tidiness. It gives me a sense of control."

"Control is important," Jewel said, "but I like it when things get a little out of hand. You know, a challenge. Like breaking a wild stallion."

Nicole had always taken small bites from life, and she envied Jewel's spirited attitude. "Is that how you handle Mace? Like a wild stallion?"

"Oh dear, you're not falling for the big lug, are you?"

"Is he seeing anyone?" Nicole asked.

"Not now. Not for a while. He's too busy taking care of the entire county to settle on any one woman."

And how might he be tamed? She doubted he could be broken because his will was far too strong. Maybe it was better to take baby steps with him. *Stop! Warning: You are approaching the seduction zone!*

She needed to forget Mace. Soon as possible, she was moving on.

The mobile telephone rang.

She gasped and stared at it. What had Mace told her to do? *Just answer.* Her conversation would be recorded. She needed to keep the kidnappers on the line as long as possible so the call could be traced.

Jewel touched her arm. "It's okay. Go ahead and pick it up."

She pressed the Talk button. "Hello?"

"Couldn't keep your big mouth shut, could you? You had to tell the sheriff."

"I'm sorry, Joey." He sounded furious, which was better than terrified. "Are you okay?"

"Is the ransom here yet?" he demanded.

"I don't know." How could she keep him on the line? "If you want to hold, I might be able to contact somebody and—"

"Don't screw this up. I'll call again later."

The phone went dead in her hand.

Chapter Six

At the airfield outside Elkhorn, Mace parked his Explorer beside the trailer-size office. This one-hangar landing strip was little more than tarmac and a wind sock, usually unmanned. But today, a half-dozen people milled around. Word had spread that the Feds were arriving today, and people in Elkhorn wanted to get a look. An FBI investigation into a kidnapping was a big deal for Sterling County.

As a matter of fact, Mace wasn't much better than the other gawkers. Nobody had invited him to the airstrip, but he'd come, nonetheless, to meet the plane carrying Agent Heflin and his FBI crew of kidnap specialists—experts in sophisticated monitoring and surveillance techniques.

Stepping out of his vehicle into the crisp October morning, Mace stretched his back and shoulders. He squinted through dark glasses at the clear-blue Colorado sky arching above foothills and conifers highlighted with frost. A good day for hunting.

For a moment, Mace was tempted to grab his camping gear and his rifle, and disappear until the FBI circus left town. That would be one way to avoid the humiliation of facing all the mistakes he'd made thus far in his investigation—including his fruitless chase of the kidnappers last night.

The New Mexico plates on the kidnapper's vehicle had proved to be another dead end. All Mace had learned from crawling on his belly through the icy shadows was that there were at least three kidnappers and they were driving a black or dark-blue Jeep Wagoneer. He couldn't even provide descriptions of the men, except that two of them were about six feet tall and one of them was dumb enough to wear a cowboy hat on top of his ski mask.

The worst aspect of last night's adventure was trying to make sense out of Nicole's behavior. Though Mace believed she was acting out of fear, he'd be hard-pressed to explain to the FBI why she shouldn't be their number-one suspect.

Inside his shearling jacket, his cell phone rang and he answered. It was Barry.

"They called," he said. "The kidnappers called Nicole."

"Could you trace the phone?"

"No luck. It was the cell phone again, and they didn't stay on the line long enough to triangulate their position."

"Did you record the call?" Mace asked.

"You bet," he said proudly. "My equipment worked like a charm. Here it is."

Mace listened while Joey berated and threatened Nicole. She tried to keep him on the line, but he disconnected too quickly.

To Barry, he said, "Play it again."

Through the cell phone, Mace listened for background noise and nuance. Joey's voice sounded aggressive and angry, not in the least bit scared. Which was consistent with his behavior last night. Joey had snapped at his supposed captors, and they hadn't needed to restrain him.

Mace's impressions were beginning to coalesce into a theory: Joey Wentworth might be a willing partner in this supposed kidnapping. He might have planned the whole thing to rip off his uncle.

"Want to hear it again?" Barry asked.

"That's enough for now," Mace said. "After I pick up Special Agent Heflin, I'll get back to you."

"Over and out," Barry said.

Mace punched in his home number and waited through six rings until Jewel picked up. "Put Nicole on the phone."

"Not until you say please, big brother."

Now was definitely not the time for Jewel to give him a hard time. "When did you suddenly get manners?"

"I'm learning from Nicole. I like her, Mace. She has this really interesting idea about controlling the little things in life, like being polite and—"

"Just put her on the phone. Please."

From a distance Mace heard the whine of a midsize turbo jet. He peered toward the north and saw sunlight glinting off the white-winged aircraft.

"Hello?" Nicole said.

"I need the names of anybody Joey hangs out with around here."

"We went over this before," she said. "Joey's a loner, and I really don't know his friends."

The jet was making its approach to the airstrip. Before the Feds landed, Mace wished he could have a substantive lead. At least a possible list of suspects.

"What about an address book?" he asked. Last

night at the cabin, he hadn't found anything with a list of names or phone numbers.

"He has a PalmPilot that he never uses. I think he keeps all his personal information at his apartment in Denver," she said. "He uses that as his legal address."

The jet taxied to a stop and circled around toward the hangar. "Think, Nicole."

"Maybe this will help," she said. "One time when I was posing for him, Joey got a phone call. He grabbed a blue sketchbook off the counter where he keeps all his paints and made a note on the inside cover."

"Good," he said. "That's a start."

"Mace, I had another contact with Joey. It was just a little while ago."

"I know. I listened to the recording." He wondered if she'd noticed anything strange in Joey's attitude. "How did you think he sounded?"

"Mad," she said. "I betrayed him."

Mace suspected the opposite was true. Joey was using her. "The Feds are here. I'll see you soon."

Pocketing his cell phone, Mace strode across the tarmac and introduced himself to Special Agent Luke Heflin. He was about six feet tall, the same height as Mace, and probably within ten pounds of Mace's weight. The dark-haired Heflin wasn't dressed in the typical FBI men-in-black suit. He wore beige corduroy trousers and a patterned ski sweater, more appropriate for a trip to a ski resort than to the farming and ranching communities near Elkhorn. He was accompanied by four other agents who busily unloaded their suitcases and equipment from the belly of the jet.

"I'd be happy to give you and your men a ride to the Wentworth cabin," Mace said.

"That won't be necessary, Sheriff. We've arranged for a van from the Elkhorn Lodge. That will be our base of operations."

He'd obviously never seen the Lodge, a dilapidated two-story stucco building that was nearly as old as the eccentric seventy-year-old woman who ran it, Libby Tynsdale.

Heflin checked his wristwatch. "The van should be here any minute."

Mace didn't feel inclined to explain that tourism wasn't a big business in Sterling County, and Libby had never felt the need to cater to her guests, who were mostly hunters and fishermen. She showed up when she wanted and sometimes not at all.

"In the meantime," Mace said, "I can bring you up-to-date on our investigation."

"Not here." Heflin glanced suspiciously at the folks hanging around the airfield. "We'll talk in your vehicle."

Behind the wheel of his Explorer, Mace turned to Heflin, who sat in the passenger seat with the window closed. The agent spoke first, "Let's get one thing straight, Sheriff. Your casual attitude might work well for local law enforcement, but it's not appropriate in this situation. This is an FBI operation, and we have procedures that have been tested and proved effective in kidnappings."

"I heard somewhere that the FBI success ratio in rescuing victims who are kidnapped for ransom is nearly sixty-five percent."

"As I said, it's effective."

"Not for the thirty-five percent who get killed,"

Mace said. "I'm not looking for a fight. I say we work together, coordinate our efforts."

"As long as you understand that this is my jurisdiction," Heflin said. "I checked you out before I came down here. When you were with the Denver police, you had a reputation for bending the rules and were written up three times for insubordination. I don't want any trouble."

"Don't give me a reason to cause any," Mace said. His good intentions for establishing a cooperative effort with Heflin were fading fast. "Are you ready to hear about the contacts we've had with the kidnappers?"

"Yes, and I'll also want a written report."

Outlining the events of last night, Mace got all the way up to the part where he followed Nicole.

Heflin interrupted, "Are you saying that the kidnappers broke into your home to leave this note?"

"We found scratches on a side door. The lock was picked."

"These guys are professionals," Heflin said. "A slick break-and-enter job. Placing bugging devices. Using an untraceable cell phone."

Mace continued his account with his pursuit of the kidnappers. "I got the license plate. It was registered to a car that had been totalled."

"What about the driver? He might be a lead."

"He died in the car wreck."

"And his plates went up for sale on the black market," Heflin said. "These guys are pros. Now tell me more about this Nicole Ferris. Did you know she has a criminal record?"

"As a juvenile," Mace said. Though he was sure that Nicole was still withholding information from him, he wasn't about to give her up to this jerk. "She's a waitress at the Elkhorn Café and a law-abiding citizen."

"I want to question her," Heflin said. "Right after we complete our forensics on the cabin."

Libby Tynsdale's ancient Volkswagen van rattled onto the tarmac and parked nose to nose with the jet. When Special Agent Luke Heflin read the Elkhorn Lodge logo printed on the side of the van, his eyes glazed. "Oh, no."

"Looks like your ride is here," Mace said cheerfully.

Gray-haired Libby hopped out of the van, planted her fists on her ample hips and bellowed, "If you guys are the FBI, get your buns in the van. I got another stop to make."

"Oh, no," Heflin repeated.

"Welcome to Elkhorn."

TAKING THE MOBILE PHONE with her, Nicole followed Jewel out to the stables to care for the horses. The long, whitewashed building with six stalls on each side was incredibly clean. The mingled scent of hay, leather and horse didn't seem at all unpleasant.

All the doors to the stalls were open, and Nicole peeked inside one of them. "Where are the horses?"

"In the pasture. It's a nice day for them to be outside."

When Jewel slid open the opposite door leading to corrals and pastures, a fat little burro trotted up to her and brayed, demanding attention.

Nicole laughed. "He's adorable."

"The silly donkey thinks he's a dog. If I let him, he'd sit on my lap. He follows me everywhere." She gestured toward a fenced-in corral between the stables and the barn. "These are my beauties."

Though Nicole knew very little about horses, she could appreciate the magnificence of these five Arabians. Their chestnut coats gleamed over muscled flanks. They looked strong, healthy and proud. "Beauties, indeed."

"And a lot of work," Jewel said.

"I can help. Tell me what to do."

Jewel pointed her toward high rubber work boots and a heavy-duty jacket. The chores involved a lot of lifting, shoveling and swabbing, which Nicole undertook with enthusiasm. She'd always been strong; waitress work can be physically demanding. And she enjoyed tromping through mud in her work boots and feeling the fresh October sunlight on her face. Activity was preferable to sitting around and waiting for the next dreaded phone call from the kidnappers.

When she sat for a moment's rest on a hay bale inside the stable, the burro came close and stared at her. His long ears twitched curiously. When she reached toward him, he stepped backward.

"Don't be scared," she said. "I won't hurt you."

But the burro flounced away. Not yet ready to be her friend. That seemed to be the story of her life. She was always the outsider, always on the move. It might have been nice to settle down here in Elkhorn, working in the healthy atmosphere of a ranch instead of in a greasy café.

Mace slammed through the door to the stable like a volcanic explosion. He wasn't wearing his Stetson or his shearling coat. In his tan sheriff's uniform with his gun and cuffs on his utility belt, his appearance was official and intimidating. His brow furrowed. His mouth was set in a snarl.

Without saying hello or acknowledging her presence, he picked up the mobile phone and flung it against the concrete stable floor with such force that the instrument shattered. "We won't need this anymore. The Feds are taking all phone calls."

"They can't." Nicole stood. A tremble went through her. "Joey wants to talk to me."

"He's got no choice. Agent Heflin is in charge."

Pacing the length of the barn and back again, Mace seemed to be trapped in a cage that was barely strong enough to contain his anger. His body tensed. He growled under his breath, "There's too damned much ego involved in this investigation. Heflin's got something to prove. He's treating me like his errand boy."

Nicole didn't want to see him like this. Nothing good ever came from rage. Too often the heat of anger had turned toward her. Her body ached from remembered blows, kindled by unchecked fury. Involuntary terror rose within her. "Stop it!"

He halted midstride and stared at her. The fire in his dark eyes burned through to her soul. She cringed away from him, fearful that he'd strike out at her. Her eyelids squeezed shut. Her hands rose to cover her face.

"I'm sorry," he said. "Nicole, I won't hurt you."

She wanted to believe him, but she'd heard those words too many times before and knew better than to trust him. Though she lowered her hands, her heart jumped hysterically inside her rib cage. She was scared. Instinctively she knew she should run away from him.

Jewel raced back into the stables. "What's going on here? Mace, what have you done?"

"I was mad," he said.

She glared at the broken cell phone on the floor. "So you threw a temper tantrum. How mature!"

His gaze focused steadily on Nicole. Though he had calmed by several degrees, she still saw the anger that might erupt at any second. "Trust me," he said. "Please."

"I'll try." She concentrated on controlling her breathing.

He glanced toward his sister. "Jewel, would you excuse us for a minute."

"Okay." With slow, dubious steps, she went back out the stable door. "If I hear any yelling in here, you're in deep trouble, Mace."

Alone with him in the stables, Nicole shivered. A little while ago she'd been so happy, playing with a burro and reveling in the good weather. Now she felt like sobbing. When would it end? When would her life be about something more than terror?

"I didn't mean to frighten you," Mace said. His voice was gentle, and she tried to believe him. "I forgot about your past. I was treating you like Jewel or one of the guys."

Ironically, that was exactly the kind of relationship she craved. True friends had the freedom to say anything to each other. With trust, there was no need to maintain tight control. "It's okay."

"It's not." Mace sat on the hay bale. His shoulders slumped. "I've made a lot of mistakes in the past few days, but this one is the worst. I can't pretend to know everything you've gone through, Nicole. But I'm guessing there's been some serious abuse."

"Good guess," she said quietly.

"And I come raging in here like a crazy man. You must have thought I was going to take my mad out on you." He looked up at her with sad, exhausted eyes. "I wouldn't hit you. Not ever."

"Nobody plans for abuse to happen," she said. "But it does."

"Not from me. I know right from wrong."

She swallowed hard. The grip of panic had begun to loosen. "I'm okay, Mace. No harm done. I accept your apology."

"I'll be more careful in the future."

Mace wanted to take her into his arms and comfort her, but he knew that behavior fit too well into the abusive pattern. First came the beating. Then the apologies. Then the making up.

If he'd rescued her from someone else, he might have been able to touch her. But in this case he was the unwitting perpetrator, and it didn't matter that he never would have harmed her. She expected him to be violent, and her perception made him guilty.

He'd never forget how she'd flinched and covered her face. As if he would hit her? My God, he felt like a thug.

She tried a smile. "Now, what's this about the FBI taking Joey's phone calls?"

"They've set up a base of operations at the Elkhorn Lodge where Libby Tynsdale is making their lives miserable. Bless her ornery soul. They've already reprogrammed the phones. Their *procedure* is to intercept all communication from the kidnappers."

"Why?"

"So they can be the negotiators."

"That's a stupid idea," she said. "There's nothing

to negotiate. Uncle Blake turns over the money, and Joey gets released.''

"That's another problem.'' Though Agent Heflin hadn't been forthcoming with any of their privileged information, Mace had gleaned a few bits of intelligence. "Blake Wentworth ran into a snag getting the cash released from Joey's trust fund. He won't have the ransom until late today. It might take until tomorrow.''

"And what happens to Joey in the meantime?''

"He waits,'' Mace said. "We all wait.''

She tucked a wisp of hair behind her ear. The color had returned to her face. "Isn't there something we can do?''

He intended to pursue his own investigation, separate from the Feds. Though that kind of attitude had earned him reprimands for insubordination when he was a police detective in Denver, he had pretty much decided to go his own course. This was his county, damn it! He couldn't just stand by and twiddle his thumbs.

The Feds were going down the wrong path, looking for professional criminals. Mace believed there was a connection closer to home. How else could he explain the screwball trail of clues at the cabin? And the theft of Nicole's savings? And Joey's demanding attitude?

"I'm going to follow up on some leads myself,'' he said.

"Let me help.''

He shook his head. "I can't take responsibility for putting you in the line of fire.''

"That's my choice,'' she said as she peeled off the muddy boots. "How do we get started?''

"The Feds want to talk to you," he said. "I told them I'd bring you to them."

Agent Heflin trusted him to transport a witness. It was a fetch-and-carry task, one step above filling their coffee mugs.

"I have an idea." A devilish grin played at the corners of her mouth. "I could tell them something misleading to throw off their investigation."

"No, no. This isn't a competition. We're all on the same side. We all want to bring Joey safely home." But he was beginning to have an idea. "Here's how you can help me. When I bring you to the cabin to be questioned, keep Heflin busy so I can take a look in Joey's studio."

"To see if you can find the sketchbook where he wrote down messages."

He nodded. "Be sure to pick up some clothes while you're at the cabin. You're staying here with us."

"I appreciate your hospitality."

Her ladylike response amused him. Only a moment ago she'd been prepared to con the FBI. "If you're ready, Nicole. We can go now."

"Let me say goodbye to your sister."

She ran toward the stable door, energetic as a colt. There were a lot of contrasts in Nicole. She had more moods than there were colors in a rainbow—all of them vivid. She was a trickster and a victim. Though she acted tough, she was also painfully vulnerable. Sometimes she talked like a prissy schoolmarm. Other times she sounded like a gun moll.

With all these different personas, which one was the truth? What would he find in her deepest heart? He knew one thing for sure. She needed to be handled with care. She wasn't a package that could be wildly ripped open, throwing the ribbons and bits of wrapping paper. She was breakable, and he sure as hell didn't want to be the man who caused her to break into a million pieces.

Coming back into the barn, she approached him gracefully. "Jewel says we should probably have some lunch before we go."

Mace glanced at his wristwatch. It was almost noon. "Does my bossy sister have some idea about what we should eat?"

Jewel appeared in the stable doorway. "For you, dog meat. Nicole and I will be having soup and salad like civilized human beings."

Mace nodded. It wouldn't hurt to give Heflin and his men a little more time to finish up the forensics at the Wentworth cabin. They'd taken enough equipment over there to build a space shuttle.

He fell into step behind his sister and Nicole as they returned to the house. As soon as they stepped inside, Nicole said, "There's one more thing, Mace. Can we put gas in my car and bring it back here? I don't want to leave it on the side of the road."

Her request seemed perfectly ingenuous, but he knew better. Nicole had the reputation of running. He didn't want to provide her with means of escape. "Why would you need your car?"

"For one thing, all my savings were stolen. I need to go back to work."

"Not until this is over," he said firmly. The grapevine in Elkhorn was already pulsating with rumors. If Nicole showed up at the café, the tabloids wouldn't be far behind. "We want to keep a low profile."

"It seems like my car is a hazard at the side of the road," she said. "All it needs is a gallon of gas."

"Give me your car keys, and I'll have one of the deputies pick it up." He couldn't very well deny her the use of her own vehicle. "But don't even think about running away. Not for one second. Not for one nanosecond."

She fluttered her eyelashes in a blatant display of fake innocence. "Trust me, Mace."

Chapter Seven

I will not run away. Nicole repeated the sentence over and over in her mind, like a mantra. She owed it to Joey to stay in Elkhorn and fulfill the kidnapper's demands.

I will not run away. On a practical level, she knew that if she tried to flee before the FBI gave their permission, she'd surely be apprehended, maybe even arrested.

I will not run away. She'd promised Mace that she wouldn't run. That seemed like the most important reason of all. Even though her instincts warned her to escape, she didn't want to disappoint him.

But her feet were itching as she rode to the cabin in the passenger seat of his Explorer. They were on their way to meet with Special Agent Heflin—not a fun date. Nicole would need every ounce of her poise and self-control to get through this FBI interrogation in one piece. She had to convince Heflin that she wasn't a suspect. At the same time, she couldn't be completely truthful and reveal her marriage to Derek. Was this the most complicated encounter she'd ever faced? Probably not.

Casting around in her mind, she recalled another

situation requiring steely control. Oddly enough it was a formal dinner event she'd attended with Derek. Those fancy occasions were always uncomfortable for her. The other women regarded her as a brainless trophy wife, and their husbands leered like starving men eyeballing a choice cut of prime rib. She hadn't wanted to go, but Derek insisted. He'd said that this was her job; the reason he married her was so she could be an appealing blond accessory on his arm.

Before they'd left the house, Derek had fastened a dazzling diamond necklace around her throat. He stood behind her as she stared at her reflection in the full-length mirror, amazed at how glamorous she was in her designer gown with her hair upswept and her makeup professionally applied. She looked like a princess.

Then Derek's caress tightened around her neck. He pressed just hard enough to close her windpipe, and he whispered into her ear. "You're mine, Nicole. Never forget that you belong to me."

Struggling to inhale, she managed to nod.

"I'm receiving an award tonight," he said. "If you embarrass me in any way, I will punish you."

He released his choke hold, and she gasped. Tears welled in her eyes, and she carefully dabbed the corners so she wouldn't ruin her makeup. "I'll make you proud, Derek."

Her behavior had been impeccable. For four long hours she'd endured catty comments and held her head high. She'd smiled at the dumb jokes from Derek's associates. When she danced with her supposedly loving husband, she'd gracefully followed his lead. For that one night she truly was as poised as a princess on the brink of execution.

Mentally she recaptured that imperious strength. In her dealings with the Feds at the Wentworth cabin, she would be regal, unshakeable and firm.

When Mace parked at some distance from the cabin, she saw two vans, a lot of yellow crime-scene tape and a couple of guys in black windbreakers with "FBI" written across their backs in big white letters. "What are they doing?"

"Making casts of the tire tracks," Mace said. "It's a waste of time since I already told them that the kidnappers were driving a black or dark-blue Jeep Wagoneer."

"I don't like them being here," she said. "Do I have any right to tell them to leave?"

"Afraid not. If they cause any damage, you can sue them after the fact."

"Oh, sure. As if anybody wins a suit against the FBI."

She hated that they could come here uninvited and paw through her life. Last night her cabin was ransacked. Now it felt like she was being violated all over again. The quiet refuge she'd shared with Joey didn't look anything like home.

"Let's go," Mace said. "Tell the truth, and you'll be fine."

"I hope so."

He reached over, clasped her hand and affectionately gave a light squeeze. His skin felt warm, and his touch reassured her. "You're not alone, Nicole. I won't let them bully you."

She believed him. For the first time in her life, she had somebody in her corner, somebody to protect her. "I'll keep an eye out for you, too."

"Just buy me enough time to take a look around

in Joey's studio for that blue sketchbook with the phone numbers.''

As he escorted her through the pine trees to the front entrance of her cabin, Mace felt as if he was leading her into the lion's den, but he wouldn't abandon her like a helpless gazelle to be ravaged by the pride of the FBI. He'd promised to keep her safe, and he meant to do exactly that.

Right at the moment, however, Nicole didn't seem to need protection. With her shoulders back and her head held high, she looked as though she could take on the world. By God, she was a beauty. He'd never known anyone like her before.

Inside the cabin she marched directly up to Heflin, introduced herself and shook his hand. ''Special Agent Heflin, have you received any other calls from the kidnappers?''

''That's none of your concern, Miss Ferris.''

''Have you straightened out the problems in obtaining the ransom?''

''Again, that's not—''

''What have you been doing?'' Disdainfully, she glared at the mess in her cabin and the clutter of his forensic equipment.

''You're in no position to ask questions,'' he said. ''You're supposed to answer to me.''

''Fine.'' She picked up a rocking chair that had been overturned, dusted off the seat and sat. ''Go ahead. Ask.''

''In case it escaped your attention, you're a suspect, Miss Ferris.''

''Why?''

''You're close to Joey. You know his schedule. You could have arranged the abduction.''

"So could anyone else," Mace pointed out. Proximity sure as hell wasn't proof of guilt. "Besides, Nicole wasn't at the cabin when her roommate was kidnapped. She was at the café, watching the Bronco game. They lost. Twenty-four to sixteen."

Heflin shot him an angry look, then turned back to Nicole. "You came back here and purposely contaminated the crime scene."

"By changing out of my wet clothing?" She scoffed. "That hardly seems nefarious."

"Why did you break the window in the bathroom?" Heflin demanded.

"I didn't." She rolled her eyes. "I'm not stupid enough to fake a break-in by shattering the glass from the wrong side."

"So you think you're smart," Heflin said. "Smart enough to stage your roommate's abduction?"

"I don't think kidnapping is a particularly clever scheme," she said. "Besides, if I'd been in charge, I would have asked for lots more ransom."

Mace frowned. Her snippy attitude was sure to provoke a more aggressive approach from Heflin. Intimidation was standard interrogation technique. Plus, the special agent wouldn't take kindly to having this delicate blonde get the best of him in Q and A.

"How much more ransom?" Heflin asked.

"Ten million."

"Why?"

She smiled. "Why not?"

"You're not so smart." Heflin grabbed the arms of her rocking chair. He got right up in her face. "Last night you ducked out of the sheriff's house to meet with the kidnappers. You collaborated with them.

They want you to deliver the ransom. I believe you're guilty, Miss Ferris.''

''Is it a crime to care about what happens to my roommate?''

''Aiding and abetting,'' Heflin said. ''Kidnapping is a capital offense. You'll do your time in a federal prison.''

Though she stared back at him with an unblinking gaze, Mace sensed a crack in her veneer of poise. Heflin was too close. His dominating physical presence breached her personal space.

In a cool voice Nicole asked, ''Are you quite finished?''

''I haven't even gotten started.''

She glanced at her wristwatch. ''Exactly how long will it take for you to assert your manhood?''

Heflin's eyes bulged as his face turned brick red. His grip on the arms of her rocking chair was white-knuckled. He looked as if he was ready to haul off and smack her upside the head.

Mace had to interrupt. ''Agent Heflin, maybe you could use a glass of water.''

''I'm not talking to you, Sheriff.''

''The altitude is a little higher here,'' Mace said. ''Looks like you're breathing hard. I wouldn't want you to keel over from a heart attack.''

When Mace touched his shoulder, Heflin sprang away from Nicole and confronted him. ''Don't you know any better than to interrupt an interrogation?''

''Is that what you call this?'' Mace kept his voice level. ''I don't see a tape recorder. I don't see you taking notes.''

''That's not how I operate.'' Heflin pointed Mace toward the kitchen. ''Step this way.''

The forensics team had left their mark in the kitchen with a faint dusting of powder for fingerprinting. On the counter, a rectangular black console with an audio level indicator and headset awaited the next call from the kidnappers.

Mace pointed to the equipment. "I think it's best to have Nicole talk with the kidnappers. She has a rapport with Joey."

"Frankly, Sheriff, I don't care what you think. This is my investigation." Heflin folded his arms across his chest and scowled. "I'm FBI trained to negotiate with kidnappers."

"Is that so?" Mace knew the statistics. Abduction for ransom was a rare occurrence within the boundaries of the continental United States. "How many cases like this have you handled?"

"A number."

And what was that number? One? Ten? Zero? "Nowadays, it seems like most kidnappings are teenagers or kids. The criminal's motivation is deviant sexual behavior. Not ransom. This situation with Joey is real old-fashioned."

"My methods are state-of-the-art." Heflin's face was still red with anger. Even the whites of his eyes were bloodshot. "In questioning Nicole, I'm using complex, psychology-based techniques for obtaining information."

What a load of bull! "How so?"

"First, I'm letting her know who's boss," Heflin said. "For your information, Nicole was a runaway, probably abused as a kid."

"So, your strategy is to terrorize her."

"I'll do whatever it takes to get information," Heflin said.

"Including abuse?" Mace was so disgusted he could spit. Either Heflin was a clueless idiot or a bully. "I sincerely hope these complex methods of yours don't include beating up a witness."

"I do what's necessary."

"Not in my county." Mace squared his shoulders, ready for a confrontation. "Did I miss something here? I thought we were still in America."

"This is my case, Sheriff. Back off."

Mace wouldn't mind getting physical. He was fairly sure he could take Mr. Complex Techniques without breaking a sweat. "You can rest assured of this, Agent Heflin. If you lay a hand on Nicole, you'll regret it."

"Whose side are you on, anyway?"

"The right side."

Mace's primary reason for coming to the cabin was to search for the notebook. He hadn't expected to encounter this extreme level of stupidity. It was definitely time to take matters into his own hands.

Leaving the kitchen, he went back to where Nicole was sitting in the rocking chair. He gently patted her arm. "I'm going to get out of the way for a while so Agent Heflin can talk to you. But if you feel the need for assistance, give a shout."

Her eyes warmed as she smiled up at him. "I'm glad you're here."

"So am I."

Leaving Heflin and Nicole, he made his way through the cabin to Joey's studio where he slipped inside and closed the door behind him. Nicole had told him that the sketchbook was on the counter under the wall of multipaned windows. Amid boxes of charcoals and helter-skelter tubes of acrylic paint, he found several blue sketchbooks of varying sizes and shapes. He flipped through the smallest one, finding a lot of doodles that made no sense and a Picasso-like rendering of a woman with four breasts. Another sketchbook seemed to be totally devoted to shadows on pine trees. In the third book, he found scribbled phone numbers on the cover.

By rights, he ought to turn this over to the Feds. *The hell he would!* Mace tore off the sketchbook cover, folded it and stuck it in his inner jacket pocket.

There might be other clues in this studio. In his paintings, Joey might have subconsciously revealed his plans. Though Mace had already taken digital photos of several of these artworks when he first investigated at the cabin, it always helped to see the real thing.

He cocked his head to stare at the hellish painting of Nicole. He didn't know much about art, but he suspected that Joey's intention was to contrast Nicole's lovely delicate face—the visage of an angel—with a demonic interior. It was a common theme. Many Ute fables spoke of evil masquerading as beauty.

But this painting was also filled with rage and hatred. There was cruelty in the way the skin had been peeled back from her fingers. Whether or not she was aware of her transgression, Nicole must have done something to make Joey mad. His artistic treatment of the other background figures was no less vicious. Mace peered closely at a satyr-looking beast. The creature's face resembled someone Mace knew. His name was Don Blackbird, and he lived southwest of Elkhorn in a little town called Las Ranas.

It might be worth a trip to hear what Don Blackbird had to say about Joey the artist.

When Mace returned to the front room of the cabin, Heflin's face was still flushed. In contrast, Nicole seemed perfectly in control, ignoring a sheaf of documents he waved beneath her nose.

"According to these records," Heflin said, "there have been several times in your life when you weren't working. How did you support yourself?"

"I'm a waitress," she said. "I might have worked for a few places that didn't keep accurate employment records."

"You didn't report your income. You defrauded the government."

"Or I might have taken a vacation."

"Who would know?" Heflin demanded. "I want names. Family and friends."

"My stepfather lives in San Francisco. I haven't seen him since I was sixteen. I have no other relations."

"I want names," Heflin repeated.

She rattled off three names and phone numbers. Two of them lived in San Francisco. The other was in Phoenix. "I'm not sure if those numbers are still good. I really don't stay in touch."

"Before you moved in with Joey, who did you work for in Denver?"

"A restaurant that went out of business." She exhaled an impatient sigh. "Why don't we cut to the chase, Agent Heflin? You want to know if I associate with known criminals. The answer is no. Never. Certainly not since I've been in Elkhorn."

"I'll be questioning the people at the Elkhorn Café," he said.

''Knock yourself out.''

''Let's go over the night of the crime again,'' he said. ''Start with when your car ran out of gas.''

As Nicole repeated her narrative, Mace wondered why Heflin hadn't pushed to find out more about her recent history. She consistently avoided questions about her time spent in Denver.

Though Mace didn't think her evasion had anything to do with Joey's kidnapping, he was curious. Something had happened to Nicole in Denver, and it was one of the keys to explaining her complicated personality—her unusual mix of a princess's poise and the street smarts of a guttersnipe.

As she completed her story, she folded her hands primly on her lap. ''Anything else?''

Heflin's wild-eyed accusations seemed to have played out. He looked spent, incapable of intimidating a chipmunk. Still, he doggedly repeated, ''Tell me again about last night when you met with the kidnappers.''

''I only saw Joey. He told me that the kidnappers want me to deliver the ransom.''

''Not going to happen,'' Heflin said. ''You won't get your pretty little hands on that money.''

''If we don't follow instructions, the kidnappers might hurt Joey. Probably they'll hurt me, too.''

Heflin said, ''I could take you into protective custody.''

''I think not.'' She jumped to her feet so quickly that the rocking chair whipped back and forth like a pendulum. ''I intend to stay with Mace's sister.''

Mace stepped up beside her. ''It's the safest place in town. I'll have deputies watching the front and back doors.''

"Last night," Heflin pointed out, "your house was broken into."

"We've secured the premises," Mace said coldly. "The ranch is safe."

"You know, Sheriff. I've warned you before about interfering." Wearily Heflin lumbered to his feet. "If you keep poking your nose where it doesn't belong, I'll have you removed."

You and what army? Mace capped his hostility before speaking. In this circumstance, it was better to be rational. "I'm trying to be helpful. Now that you've seen the accommodations at the Elkhorn Lodge, you'll probably agree that they aren't particularly conducive to protective custody."

"The Lodge," Heflin muttered. "The place is a pigsty run by a crazy woman."

"And you probably don't want to waste the time of your expert crew on bodyguard duty," Mace said.

"We'd be better off moving our base of operations to this cabin."

"In which case, you don't want a woman taking up one of the bedrooms." Mace turned to Nicole. "Go pack a few of your things and we'll head back to the ranch. Be quick."

As she darted toward her former bedroom at the cabin, Mace almost pitied Special Agent Heflin. He'd expected a classy mountain lodge, and he got Libby Tynsdale instead. Nicole wasn't the easily intimidated witness he'd expected. And the kidnappers still hadn't called back. Sometimes investigations don't work out as neatly as in the movies.

Heflin sank into the rocking chair Nicole had vacated. "She's involved in this, Sheriff. I'm not sure how. But she's a suspect."

"I'll keep an eye on her," Mace promised. "You have my phone number in case you need to be in touch."

Nicole raced out of her bedroom carrying a few clothes in her arms and a gym bag that she hadn't bothered to zip. Her haste to escape Heflin and his questions was obvious. She charged directly to the front door. "Bye, Agent Heflin."

"Hold it!" Heflin hauled himself out of the rocking chair in a halfhearted attempt to reestablish his authority. "Don't leave town, Miss Ferris."

Chapter Eight

Nicole was out the door, dodging through the pine trees on her way back to Mace's Explorer. A cool sense of relief flowed through her. She'd gotten through the interrogation without falling apart. She hadn't been flustered, frightened and furious. Not a failure, she was…fine.

Mace unlocked the car door for her, and she scrambled inside with her clothes and gym bag clutched in her arms. Safely in the passenger seat, she beamed at him.

"You did great," Mace said. "Your comment about Heflin's manhood might not have been the best way to get into his good graces, but—"

"I wasn't trying to win a popularity contest."

"Don't worry. Nobody would call you Miss Congeniality."

As they drove away from the cabin, she stowed her gym bag in the back seat. "Heflin isn't going to let me take the kidnapper's calls, is he?"

"Nope."

"And he's for sure not going to let me deliver the ransom."

"Not a chance," Mace said.

"I can live with that."

She settled back in the passenger seat and relaxed. Through the windshield she viewed the wide-open Western landscape, unfettered by the complexities of cities. In this vast plain, bordered by foothills and snow-capped peaks, she was a tiny speck—hardly bigger than a tumbleweed—who could easily disappear and never be missed. Unless, somehow, she made her mark on this land.

Mace drove past the turnoff to his ranch house.

"Whoa, there, cowboy. Where are we going?"

"To visit a demon."

She might have been worried, but he was grinning. "A demon?"

"When I was in Joey's studio, I noticed something about that graveyard painting."

"The one with me as Queen of the Damned?" She shuddered, wishing she could forget that disturbing image.

"You weren't the only one in the picture," he said. "One of the demons had the face of someone I know. His name is Don Blackbird. Does that ring a bell for you?"

She thought for a moment, then shook her head. It was an unusual name—one she would have remembered. "Never heard of him."

"He's active with the commercial side of the Ute tribe. His father helped set up the pottery factory. Don is involved in the reservation casinos. I think I know where to find him."

"So we're going to pay him a visit," she said, "to see what he knows about Joey."

"And I wanted you to come along to see if you recognize him." He reached into his jacket pocket and took out the cover of the blue sketchbook. "Take a look at these names and phone numbers. See if there's anything familiar."

Concentrating intently, she deciphered Joey's scribbles and read several names aloud. "There's a George and Mark. And Jimbo."

"Any phone prefixes?"

"Some are Denver and some are here." But none of the names and numbers jumped out at her. Her fingers touched the imprints, trying to read them like Braille, wishing she could turn these random scratchings into something significant. "What are you going to do with these names?"

"I'll turn them over to Barry. He'll track them down and see if any of these guys have criminal records."

"Shouldn't you have given this clue to the Feds?"

"That would have been correct procedure."

Behind his dark glasses, his expression was masked, and she couldn't tell what he was thinking. "Is there a reason you're deviating from correct procedure?"

"Let's just say that I have a different theory from Heflin's. He thinks the kidnapping was done by professionals. I don't."

Nicole understood. From the very start of this investigation—even when they assumed it was only a robbery—Mace believed Joey was involved in the crime. Apparently, he was now setting out to prove his hypothesis. It was an arrogant decision, but she thoroughly approved. If anyone could find these kidnappers and rescue Joey, it was Mace. "I'm glad you're investigating on your own."

"I've got nothing to lose but my pride. And everything to gain. We might find Joey."

"Mace's law," she said. "You don't mind going outside the rules."

"Look who's talking."

She almost laughed out loud. Together, they made the most unlikely pair of rebels: a straight-arrow sheriff and a runaway trophy wife.

Their unspoken camaraderie gave her a sense of belonging. He trusted her enough to share his investigation with her. "Tell me about the Ute side of your family."

"My mother was half Ute. I never knew my grandmother, but my grandfather was Charlie Brook, a silversmith who lived on the rez. I called him Tata Charlie."

"Did he make your necklace?"

Mace reached up and touched the silver bear that rested in the hollow of his throat. "A bear totem. He gave it to me after a powwow when I participated in the bear dance."

"The one where the girls ask the boys to dance," she said.

"It's more significant than that. Kind of like coming of age. The bear stands for strength."

"And protection," she said, thinking of how a ferocious grizzly takes care of its young. "Very appropriate for you."

She wondered what his life had been like, growing up with one foot in each world. His sienna skin tone and nearly black eyes would have set him apart. Had he felt lonely? Different?

While working at the Elkhorn Café, Nicole wasn't able to tell the difference among the many racial blends of Native American and Latino in this area. But the locals knew at a glance. "Was there prejudice when you were growing up?"

"Why do you ask?"

"I'm sorry," she said quickly. "I didn't mean to be insulting."

"No offense taken." He glanced over at her. "Your question seems kind of intimate—like something a girlfriend might ask on a first date."

"Or something a sheriff might ask in an interrogation," she said. "It seems only fair that I should know about your background. After all, you know all about me."

"Do I?"

She wasn't going down that path again. "Until I moved to Elkhorn, I always lived in cities. I never met anyone like you or Jewel."

"Jewel and I were lucky. Being of mixed race was never a big problem for us because our dad was completely accepting of the Ute culture. He encouraged us to learn about our family on the rez. I guess we had the best of both worlds. On the ranch we got to play cowboys. On the reservation we were Indians."

"Tell me about your mother."

He smiled gently. "A smart woman. *Squaw* sounds like a derogatory term, but women have status among the Utes. They were the ones who kept the villages running and successful."

"While the men were out hunting?"

"Or putting on war paint for a raid," he said sarcastically. Then he threw back his head and gave a piercing war cry. "Yi-yi-yi-yi."

Surprised, she gaped at him. This was the second time she'd seen the unleashed side of this usually self-possessed man. The first was in the stable when he was angry and had frightened her. Now, he was laughing, full of engaging energy and strength.

"Do that again," she said.

"Do it with me," he urged.

"I simply couldn't."

"Chicken?"

She threw back her head. "Yi-yi-yi-yi-yi."

Laughter bubbled through her as she leaned back on the seat. She wouldn't have minded if this ride had been a date, if they'd been together just because they wanted to be.

Mace glanced over at her. "That's the simple explanation of what it's like to be Ute. It's not the textbook pictures of teepees and papooses and bows and arrows. It's freedom to be yourself. Being Ute is my identity, my heritage, my tribe."

His life was so different from hers. Nicole had almost no family or guidance while growing up. Mace had an entire tribe. Two tribes, the ranchers and the people on the rez. "Why did you leave Elkhorn for Denver?"

"It was a quest," he said. "I needed to go far away to discover that my life was really here."

Again, she was struck by the disparity between them. She was unconnected, a thistle on the wind. Mace had roots. "Now that you know you belong here, would you ever leave again?"

"Sure. But I'd probably always come back."

Mace slowed as they drove by the road sign for Las Ranas. They passed a few ramshackle houses and cruised through the little town in about four minutes flat. Just beyond the stop sign, Mace parked outside a tavern. The two-story, wood-frame structure had a covered porch where two old men sat and stared at the road. Beside them was a sleeping yellow dog.

Nicole read the sign beside the door. "Espresso. Latte. Beer. Soda pop. And worms. Oh, yum."

"Don't order the coffee," Mace warned.

"I thought I might have a cup of worms."

"You'd be better off."

Inside the tavern, the afternoon sunlight through the windows facing west provided a fading glow on scarred, ancient hardwood floors. A handful of people sat at the long bar and at tables.

Mace led her to a table by the windows looking out at the parking lot. No sooner were they seated than a long-legged blond woman who didn't look old enough to be working in a bar bounced over to them.

"Sheriff Mace!" She giggled. "It's been a while."

When he introduced Daisy, she grabbed Nicole's fingers and pumped in a bone-rattling handshake. "I know you. Elkhorn Café?"

"That's right," Nicole said.

"I never forget a face." Daisy turned back to Mace. "Is Nicole your new girlfriend?"

He leaned back in his chair, removed his sunglasses and grinned. "Maybe she is."

Nicole swallowed hard. Unless her ears were deceiving her, Mace claimed that she might be his girlfriend. This afternoon was definitely beginning to feel more like a date than an investigation.

"Good," said Daisy. "It's about time you settled down and got married, Mace."

Married? Nicole was stunned.

Surely he'd put a stop to this nonsense. But when she glanced toward him, his dark-eyed gaze rested coolly upon her. In contrast, she felt feverishly hot.

Daisy rattled on, "When you two decide to get hitched, let me do the catering. It'll be the biggest party we've ever had in Sterling County."

Mace grinned. "You sound just like your mother, Daisy."

"Do not! Mama is interfering. I'm interested."

Nicole needed to derail this marriage rumor before it built up a full head of steam and roared through the county. Such gossip could only lead to a train wreck. "Daisy," she said, "Mace and I aren't really considering marriage."

"But you're together."

Nicole felt flustered. "This isn't a date. We haven't even kissed."

"Well, you could change that right now," she said.

"What do you mean?"

"Hello? It's obvious," Daisy said.

She grabbed Mace's arm and pulled him from his chair. Then she did the same with Nicole. They were standing face-to-face.

"Go ahead," Daisy urged. "Kiss him."

What was going on? Was this some kind of bizarre Sterling County rite of passage? As Nicole looked up at Mace, the pressure built inside her. All the rotten memories of prior relationships surged to the forefront of her mind. She wasn't over Derek. Even though the physical bruises had faded, she wasn't ready to trust another man. Not even Mace. Not even for a simple little kiss. "I will not kiss him."

"Your choice," Daisy said. "I know fifty women who would give a hundred bucks to be standing in your shoes right now."

Mace said nothing. He waited for her to make the

first move. Even now, when his masculine reputation was on the line, he didn't push, didn't make demands.

She was making a big deal over nothing. What would it hurt to kiss him? It wasn't as if this relationship had a chance of becoming…a relationship.

Nicole rested her hand on his warm cheek. She went up on tiptoe, intending to lightly brush her lips against his. But when she tasted his mouth, she lingered too long.

Mace clasped his arm around her waist, holding her firmly but gently. His mouth moved against hers, and she felt a sizzle of excitement. The heat of his body set fire to her skin. Delicious flames licked through her—awakening and sensually arousing her.

Then their kiss ended.

Nicole was aware that the other people in the tavern were cheering. She felt embarrassed, but in a good way.

"I knew you two were right for each other," Daisy said. "Mace needs a woman who can stand up to him."

And she needed a man who could stand up *for* her, who could support her no matter what. Nicole searched the depths of his eyes—dark pools reflecting his strength and caring. Was he the man she needed? She sank back into her chair, not daring to hope. Too many of her dreams had been trampled and crushed. She couldn't bear another disappointment.

"Now," Daisy said, "can I get you both some coffee? On the house."

"Not coffee," Mace said quickly. "Orange soda."

As he returned to his seat, Nicole studied him. In a low voice, she asked, "Why did that happen?"

"I'm not sure."

Mace wished he could explain. He hadn't planned to kiss her. Sure, he could come up with excuses, could say that he didn't want to introduce her as a witness, and it was easier to pretend that they were dating. But that glib rationalization didn't explain why he had kissed her back.

The truth was simple. He wanted to kiss her. Maybe he'd wanted to kiss her from the first moment he saw her.

"I feel a little silly," she said.

"Me, too." He was tongue-tied. Obviously, he'd been out of the dating scene too long. He couldn't even remember what a smooth move looked like.

"I'm not sorry I kissed you," she said. "But it won't happen again."

"If you change your mind," he said. "I'm ready whenever you are."

"What if it's not for weeks?"

"I'll wait," he said.

"What if I'm gone tomorrow?"

"Then we'll never know what might have been."

He studied her angelic face. A pink blush colored her cheeks. The intriguing sparkle in her blue eyes was like the shimmer of sunlight on a waterfall. Her wide mouth curved in one of her infrequent smiles, and he was glad that he'd put that grin on her face.

When Daisy returned to the table with their drinks, Mace dragged his focus back to the investigation. "I'm looking for Don Blackbird. Has he been around today?"

"He just left, but he's coming back. So you might as well wait. I'll bring chips and salsa."

She bounded toward the bar, bursting with energy

in this wild little tavern. Mace gave an exasperated sigh as he watched her. "Daisy's a blond tornado."

"What's her story?" Nicole asked.

"Her parents own the deed to the tavern, but Daisy always considered this to be her place. Ever since she was a kid, she was always dashing in and out. Now she's trying to class it up. The espresso machine is her idea."

Nicole asked, "Is it true that she always remembers people?"

"Like all gossips, she's great with names."

"Maybe she knows Joey."

He hadn't considered that possibility, but it was likely. When Daisy returned with their chips, he said, "I'm also looking for Joey Wentworth. Do you know him?"

"The guy who was kidnapped?"

Mace didn't bother asking how she knew about the abduction. "Have you seen him?"

"I'm not quite sure who he is. What does he look like?"

Nicole said, "He's five-nine. Shaggy brown hair. Goofy-looking smile. And he's always got paint stains on his hands and clothes."

"The artist," Daisy said. "Sure, I know him. He used to set up his easel over by Boot Hill Cemetery."

"Have you seen him in the past few days?" Mace asked.

"Nope." Daisy frowned and shook her head. "I can't believe he was kidnapped. I never would have guessed he was rich."

"You know, Daisy. It'd be a real help to me if anybody who happened to see Joey in the past few days would contact me."

"I'll put out the word." Still shaking her head, she left their table and slipped behind the bar where she chatted with another patron who turned and talked to someone else. Just by watching, Mace could observe the spread of information. The Feds might have state-of-the-art surveillance and recording equipment, but the gossip grapevine was a faster way to circulate information.

"Amazing," Nicole said as she noted the same phenomenon. "You just started a county-wide search."

"Maybe some results will turn up. Somebody noticing the kidnappers. Can't hurt."

"Not like the rumor about our supposed dating," she said. "By the time we get back to the ranch house, Jewel will be picking flowers for my bridal bouquet."

"By that time," he said, "the rumor mill will have you pregnant with twins."

Her smile widened. "This never happened to me before. I've always been anonymous."

"Not anymore," he said. "You're a Sterling County celebrity."

"I can't think of anything else I'd rather be."

Mace spotted Don Blackbird coming through the door and waved him over to their table. Blackbird was a big man, as husky as the kidnappers he'd seen in ski masks. He was tough and smart enough to pull off the abduction of Joey Wentworth, but Mace doubted Blackbird would bother. His holdings in the Four Corners area casinos paid him a decent living.

When he introduced Nicole, Blackbird nodded, then frowned at her. "I know you from the paintings," he said. "Joey said you were his lady."

"We're roommates," she said.

"Joey said you'd take off all your clothes to pose for him, and he'd paint on your body."

She rolled her eyes. "Joey has a vivid imagination. I never posed nude for him."

Mace turned to Don Blackbird. "I recognized your face in some of Joey's artwork. Did you pose naked?"

"You think I took my clothes off for a guy?" His big shoulders shuddered. "I'm not that way."

The grimy ring around his shirt collar and smudges on his jeans told Mace that Don Blackbird probably didn't often remove his clothes—not even for a bath. "But you and Joey were friends."

"Not really." Blackbird's forehead wrinkled as he considered. "He liked to talk about ghostwalkers in the cemetery. He called them zombies."

Nicole nodded her head. "The first time I met Joey was in a cemetery. He's been obsessed with death since his parents were killed in a plane crash outside Aspen."

"That's right," Don Blackbird said. "Joey's an orphan."

"What else can you tell me about him?" Mace asked.

"Not much. I let him paint my picture. Just my face. Sometimes I saw him in the casinos."

"Joey was a gambler," Mace said.

"A bad gambler. He got into private poker games and owed a lot of money."

"How much?"

"Thousands," Blackbird said. "Maybe ten or twenty."

Mace would've preferred to hear that Joey owed

hundreds of thousands. An astronomical debt would be motivation to stage his own kidnapping. "Was anybody threatening Joey?"

"Enough to kidnap him?" The lazy grin vanished as Blackbird leaned forward on the table. "Listen, Mace, I play no part in this. I thought maybe you'd make a connection to me, but I got nothing to do with a kidnapping."

"Why did you think I'd make a connection to you?"

"From the paintings," he said. "I know Joey. But that's all."

"Tell me who else knows Joey."

"I'm not a snitch."

Mace could have arrested him, but it wouldn't do any good. "Can you think of anything that would help me find Joey?"

"No," he said.

Mace believed him. The only useful information he'd get from Don Blackbird was that Joey was in need of ready cash. "You know how to contact me if you hear anything."

"Sure thing, Mace." He stood, nodded to Nicole, and strolled toward the bar.

When Mace turned back toward Nicole, he saw all the color drain from her face. Still as a statue, she stared through the window at the parking lot. She looked as if she'd seen a ghost.

Chapter Nine

She saw Derek. In the parking lot outside the tavern, she saw him walking toward a dark sedan with tinted windows. Nicole recognized his heavy shoulders in the Armani leather jacket he'd worn so many times before. On the back of his head, she saw the bald spot in his thinning brown hair.

Without turning toward her, he climbed into the passenger seat and closed the car door. She hadn't seen him clearly, hadn't seen his face, but she knew it was him. No one else could inspire this heart-wrenching terror. She couldn't breathe. Her pulse went dead.

Her eyes stared, unblinking, as the car drove away. He was gone.

Her frantic gaze searched the gravel parking lot off the two-lane main road through Las Ranas. It seemed inconceivable that the sun was still shining and the sky was still blue in a world that had exploded. One glimpse of Derek and she was destroyed. Ravaged by fear, she watched as the yellow dog that had been sleeping on the porch loped toward the red stop sign.

Had she really seen him? Rationally, she knew that

Derek couldn't have been here. There was no earthly reason for him to come to Las Ranas.

"Nicole?"

She heard Mace's voice, calling her back to reality, but her throat was momentarily paralyzed and she couldn't respond.

"Nicole, are you all right?"

She forced herself to inhale and exhale. Her heart started beating again. "I'm fine."

Her mouth was dry, parched as a desert. But when she reached for the orange soda, her hand shook too much to lift the glass to her lips.

Mace captured her trembling fingers. "You saw something. Joey?"

"No."

"Look at me, Nicole."

Her gaze lifted, and she was rewarded with the sight of Mace's handsome face. Sincere concern etched his features as he studied her intently, and she suddenly understood why she'd conjured up Derek. Her vision of the abusive man who wrecked her life was a subconscious message. Nicole must never forget that she wasn't the sort of woman who was destined for a healthy relationship...not even with a county sheriff who seemed to embody all the traits of a truly good man. It would never work. There could be no happy endings for her.

"I thought I saw someone," she said. "Someone from my past."

"Who?"

"It doesn't matter because he wasn't really there. I imagined him. Sounds a little crazy." More than a *little* crazy. "There's a psychological label for this.

What do the shrinks call it when you see people who aren't there?''

"Paranoid," he said.

"That's me." Though she tried to shrug it off, her muscles were too clenched to move. "Paranoid."

"You're not crazy, Nicole. You're having a natural reaction to a high-stress situation."

Then why hadn't she felt the stress earlier? She'd enjoyed her conversation with Mace on the drive down here. Their shared war cry was fun. It was only after they kissed that she saw a vision of Derek.

"This imaginary person," he said. "It wasn't Joey, was it?"

"No. I'm not scared of Joey."

"Maybe you should be."

She shook her head. Her panic had begun to subside. The more she talked, the less hysterical she felt. As long as she remembered that there could never be a real relationship for her, she'd be fine.

"Listen, Mace, I know your theory is that Joey staged his own kidnapping. But I don't believe it."

"We just heard from Don Blackbird that Joey had gambling debts. That's a motive."

"Ten or twenty thousand dollars isn't enough to risk capital punishment. He could have gotten the money from his uncle Blake."

"What if Uncle Blake turned him down?"

Daisy bounced back over to their table. "Look at you two holding hands. Just remember that I'm catering the wedding."

Nicole released her grasp on Mace's long, brown fingers. No wedding. No way. She grabbed the glass of orange soda and drained it.

"Can I bring you anything else?" Daisy asked. "It's almost dinnertime."

"We've got to leave," Mace said. "Thanks for everything, Daisy."

When he stood, he placed a twenty on the table. Daisy deserved a good tip. If she hadn't been so pushy, he never would have kissed Nicole, and that was a moment he would never regret.

He helped her into her red parka and pulled her long flaxen braid out from the collar. The smooth texture of her hair slipped through his hand. Someday he would unfasten that plait and tangle his fingers in the silken length.

"Are we going back to the ranch?" she asked.

"I want to make a stop by Boot Hill on the way back. To get an idea of what Joey was painting."

When he rested his hand on her back to guide her toward the exit, she scooted quickly ahead as though she wanted to avoid his touch. Her attitude had changed from lighthearted to guarded.

Whatever she had seen outside the tavern spooked her to the core. She'd been terrified. Mace had felt the trembling in her ice-cold hands.

Back in the Explorer, he checked in with dispatch for an update on the kidnapping. As he drove on the road leading back to Elkhorn, he passed on the information to Nicole, "The kidnappers still haven't called back. And Blake Wentworth isn't scheduled to arrive until tomorrow."

"Does he have the ransom money?" she asked.

"He'll have it by eight o'clock tomorrow morning. I'm not sure whether he's raiding Joey's trust fund or receiving a payment through his insurance company. But he'll have cash."

"Good," she said. "This ought to be over soon."

Then what? Would she leave? "I hope when the investigation is wrapped up, you'll stick around."

"Why?"

"Because I'd like to know you better."

"Same here, but…" Her voice trailed off.

"Think about it." He turned off the main road and followed a twisting road across an open plain. Boot Hill Cemetery was located halfway between Elkhorn and Las Ranas on a small rise above a streambed that was dry at this time of year.

As Mace parked and exited the car, he looked up at skies streaked with the red and gold reflections of the setting sun. Dusk came early in October. "Let's hurry," he said. "I don't want to be here after dark."

She stood beside him. The last rays of sunlight burnished her cheeks. "Tell me about Boot Hill."

"Back in the old days, people used to bury their dead on their ranches or farms. Boot Hill was for townspeople who didn't own land. Or for those who had no friends or family. Probably no one has been buried here for seventy years." He pointed toward a ravine that was roughly fifty yards away. "This site is doubly sacred. A Ute chief was supposed to be buried over there."

"Did the Utes have burial grounds?"

He led the way across a rickety wooden bridge that spanned the dry streambed. "My tribe isn't always ritualistic about disposing of the body, but they believe in immortality. After death, two spirits battle for the soul. The good spirit usually wins and the dead person is welcomed to the happy hunting ground. When the evil spirit wins, the soul is doomed to walk the earth."

"A ghostwalker. Like Don Blackbird said."

Mace climbed the worn stairs leading to a weathered picket fence surrounding the headstones and markers. At the far end of the small graveyard, the bare branches of two cottonwood trees were silhouetted against the sunset. A cold wind whispered across the forlorn landscape. He didn't like this place; nothing good could happen here. "Why did Joey want to paint a cemetery?"

"I kind of like graveyards," she said. "They're peaceful."

Nicole strolled through the gate. She leaned down to read the name on a worn wooden marker. Her finger traced the letters. Almost without thinking, she pulled a few dead weeds to tidy the gravesite. She went to another grave and did the same.

"What are you doing?" Mace asked.

"Honoring the dead. It makes me sad when people who have died are neglected. You know, if I'd died here a hundred years ago, I'd be in Boot Hill."

He got the point—she had no family, no friends, no land—but he didn't like the image. "You wouldn't have been alone. A hundred years ago, there's no way a healthy young woman like you would have been unmarried."

"I might have chosen to be single."

"You'd have a thousand suitors knocking at your door. One of them would convince you."

"A thousand suitors, huh?" She moved away from him and focused on a crumbling tombstone. "Look at this thing. All alone and forgotten. The dead need to pass on their memories. I think of my father and mother every day of my life. It keeps them alive."

She wandered through the markers, reading off the

names and dates. Her red parka and golden hair were
the only splashes of color in this arid land of death.
He had an urge to pull her away from here and take
her to a warm, vibrant place where she might grow
and flourish. The seeds were there. In her. But he
knew Nicole would blossom only when she was
ready.

Mace walked at the perimeter of the graveyard, trying to find the perspective Joey had used to paint this
scene. In one corner, the dried weeds and grasses
were bent and broken. Mace studied the area and dis-
covered a discarded tube of acrylic paint.

This was where Joey had stood. What had he been
thinking? Possibly, like Nicole, he found solace in the
graveyard. But his paintings showed rage and violence, as if he came here to engage demons and
ghostwalkers.

A shudder bristled the hairs at the nape of Mace's
neck. He wasn't generally superstitious, but he had a
bad feeling about Boot Hill.

The cell phone inside his jacket trilled, and he answered. It was Heflin, and he sounded angry.

"We had a call from the kidnappers," he said.

"Were you able to trace it?" Mace asked.

"They got off too fast to triangulate their position.
But they're in this general area," Heflin muttered.
"They said they'd only talk to Nicole."

No wonder he was ticked off. Heflin had made it
clear that he was in charge of negotiations. Mace said,
"I can have her back at the cabin in half an hour."

"Don't bother. Their next call will be tomorrow at
ten o'clock with instructions for the drop-off."

"I'll be there with Nicole," Mace said.

"Frankly, Sheriff, I don't trust this woman. There

are too many holes in her background. She's got no friends, no family. It's like she was dropped in Elkhorn from another planet.''

Mace watched as she came toward him. Her gait was lithe and athletic. Her head tilted as if to ask a question. Her eyes were solemn.

''Another planet,'' Mace said. ''Is that your theory? Joey was abducted by aliens?''

''Might as well have been. Forensics came up empty. There are no fingerprints in the cabin, except for Joey and Nicole. No footprints, either.''

Mace drew the logical conclusion. ''The kidnappers didn't enter the cabin.''

''Excuse me, Sheriff. That's a little naive. These guys are pros. They wore gloves and protective coverings on their shoes. Maybe plastic suits. We're dealing with a sophisticated gang who knows better than to leave clues.''

Mace wasn't about to argue with this jerk, but it was obvious to him that the damage in the cabin— including the theft of Nicole's money—had been done by Joey. He created the crime scene, then walked out the door and met his supposed abductors.

''I'll see you tomorrow morning,'' Mace said.

''Bring Nicole with you.''

Mace disconnected the call.

She stood directly in front of him. Her delicate eyebrows pinched with worry. ''That was Heflin?''

''He had a call from the kidnappers,'' Mace said. ''Seems they only want to talk to you.''

She groaned. ''Why? What do they want from me?''

He ticked off the answers they both knew already. ''They're sure you aren't a cop. They know you care about Joey. They expect you to do whatever it takes to get him back in one piece.''

Another reason took shape in the back of his mind. If Joey was part of the kidnapping scheme, he might have a personal agenda—some kind of rage against Nicole that he wanted to play out.

Mace didn't like that possibility. Joey's behavior was an unknown, uncontrolled factor. He posed a threat to Nicole.

''It isn't fair.'' She stomped toward the gate in the picket fence.

''I'm with you,'' he said. ''You shouldn't have to deliver the ransom money.''

''I could refuse to take part in this. After all, I'm just a private citizen.'' She paused at the gate, then slowly turned and gazed at the weathered graves of Boot Hill. ''But I can't walk away from Joey.''

Her loyalty to a man she considered to be nothing more than a roommate amazed him. In spite of her insistence that she was alone in the world, Nicole was a good person to have as a friend.

AFTER A PLEASANT DINNER at the ranch house with Mace and Jewel, Nicole went to her bedroom. She stood at the window, staring out and considering her options. Parked in front of the house was her blue Ford Escort, all gassed up and ready to roll. Unfortunately, two deputies were patrolling outside, and their car blocked the driveway.

There was no escape. She was stuck here for the night. And tomorrow morning she'd talk to the kidnappers and walk into certain danger delivering the ransom.

Still fully dressed, she perched on the edge of the

bed. Her nerves were strung tight as piano wire. Too tense to sleep. Too trapped to escape.

Her gaze rested on the small framed wedding photograph of her parents that she'd brought from the cabin. She wished so much that they could be here to reassure her and keep her safe. When her father was alive, he kissed the tip of her nose every night before she fell asleep and whispered, "Sleep tight. Don't let the bedbugs bite."

As a child, her only fear was imaginary bedbugs. Now she was a raving paranoid.

Nicole picked up the leather-bound diary where she had recorded her last days with her mother. Scattered among Nicole's thoughts were notes written in her mother's own hand.

There was a knock on the door, and Jewel popped her head inside. "Do you have everything you need for the night?"

"Your hospitality is perfect," Nicole said. "I really appreciate staying here."

"Worried about tomorrow?"

"I'm nervous as a tom turkey on Thanksgiving."

"Would you like some company?"

"If it's convenient for you," Nicole said.

"I've already put the horses to bed." Jewel eased into the room and sat in the chair beside a small desk. She nodded to the book in Nicole's hand. "Catching up on your reading?"

"I've memorized every page. It's a diary I kept after my mother had a stroke and couldn't talk. She wrote in this book. I always felt like she hung on for a few more days because she wanted to give me advice." Nicole gazed down at the diary. "Here's one thing she said: Don't be afraid to ask for help. Be ready to give in return.''

Jewel's smile was gentle and understanding. ''Your mother sounds like a wise woman.''

''How about this one: Never marry for money.'' Nicole's laugh was bitter. She'd certainly messed up on that one. Derek had been rich as a prince—the prince of darkness.

''My mother was like that, too. She gave a lot of advice about men. None of which I followed.''

''You never married?'' Nicole asked.

''I came close a couple of times, but I like my horses better.''

''My mother made mistakes of her own.'' Nicole read another passage, ''She wrote, 'I screwed up twice. My good husband died. The bad one was the death of me.'''

''Ouch, that's a little dark,'' Jewel said. ''There are a lot of decent men out there. You have to be willing to peel through all the layers, like with an onion.''

''They're still stinky, and they make you cry.''

''Talk about smelling bad,'' Jewel said. ''There was this one guy I dated who thought that if he took a bath more than once a week, he'd wash away his vital manly juices. Whatever that means.''

Nicole had a few bizarre dating stories of her own. For over an hour she and Jewel swapped tales and giggled like a couple of teenagers at a slumber party. It had been a very long time since she'd had a female friend to confide in.

''You remind me of someone I grew up with,'' Nicole said. ''A best friend. She was the only one I could really talk to. Without her, I'm sure I would have gone completely crazy in my teens.''

"What happened to her?"

"She moved, and we lost touch." Nicole hadn't thought of her best friend in a while. "Thanks for being here. I actually think I might sleep tonight."

Jewel stood, stretched and came toward her for a warm hug. "I'm here whenever you need me."

When she left, Nicole sighed. Maybe the world wasn't such a desolate place after all. There was always room for laughter, kindness and friends.

She hummed as she got ready for bed. After a shower, she slipped into her cozy flannel nightie, brushed her long hair and fastened it on top of her head with a clip. As soon as she pulled the comforter up to her chin, she was asleep.

Her dreams were restless. She found herself in that half-awake state when you know you're dreaming but can't stop. She was running through a mist. The earth beneath her feet felt soggy. Each step was an effort. She didn't know why, but she had to keep going, fast as she could. To escape. She had to run. Demons and ghostwalkers breathed down her neck.

Then she was at Boot Hill. A blood-red sky burned away the mist. The dark, bare branches of the cottonwoods clawed at the heavens. A filmy white form hung from a low branch.

She didn't want to come closer but couldn't stay away. The wind screamed through the tree branches as she looked up. The filmy white thing was a body hanging from a noose. The face was her own.

A cry tore from her throat, and she sat up on the bed, wide awake in the dark, disoriented. Where was she? Nothing was familiar. Was she safe?

She groped for the bedside lamp and turned it on. Soft light bathed the comfortable surroundings. She was in the guest bedroom at the ranch house of Jewel and Mace.

He came through her bedroom door. "What's wrong?"

"Only a nightmare. Nothing to worry about."

"The hell it's not."

He closed the bedroom door and strode barefoot across her bedroom to the bathroom. Awakened from sleep, he wore only a pair of gray sweatpants. His chest was bare.

He returned from the bathroom with a glass of water. In his other hand he held his automatic pistol. "Take a drink."

She held the glass in both hands and brought it to her lips. The cool liquid tasted of reality. "I'm sorry. I didn't mean to wake you."

"I'm the one who's sorry," he said. "You shouldn't have to go through this. There's no way you should be expected to talk to kidnappers and deliver ransoms. That's my job."

"Is it?"

"You bet." He sat on the edge of her bed. Though his presence was overpoweringly masculine, she didn't feel threatened. "As of now, you're free. I won't let you put yourself in harm's way."

She started to protest. "But Joey—"

"The kidnappers want money. There's no need to terrorize you." His dark eyes shone with concern. The lids slowly blinked as though he was not yet completely awake. "Now, tell me about your bad dream."

"It was a silly nightmare. It didn't make sense."

"Still, it's good to talk about it. You can tell me, then forget about it."

She took another sip of water. "Something was after me. Maybe one of those ghostwalkers."

He nodded. "Go on."

"I was at Boot Hill." Fear started rising up in her again. She placed the water glass on the bedside table. "The sky was red, like an open wound. A body was hanging from a tree branch. I saw the face. It was me." A violent shudder went through her. "Oh God, I don't want to die."

"It's okay to be scared."

He reached toward her, and she clung to his arm. She'd always been alone with her fear. It felt strange to accept his reassurance. "I don't want to hurt anymore."

She nestled against his firm, smooth chest. Her arms encircled him, and she hung on tight. Another tremble convulsed her body. Tears would have been a relief, but her emotions were tightly snarled. She could only gasp.

Mace stroked between her shoulder blades. "I won't let anybody hurt you."

Though his promise seemed impossible, she believed him. He was strong and good. He would protect her. For long moments she clung to him. Gradually her screaming fears became quiet. Her muscles released their fierce tension. Her grip loosened.

She leaned back to look into his face. He was her rescuer, the one good man who could make up for all the evil in the world. "Thank you," she whispered.

"You're beginning to trust me." He gently brushed the hair off her face. "I'm glad."

"So am I." She studied the arch of his eyebrow, the fullness of his lips, the smooth sienna tone of his skin. Nicole was suddenly, surprisingly aware that she was in bed with a very sexy man.

And she wanted to please him.

She lay back on the pillows with one arm thrown up over her head. A flannel nightgown wasn't the slinkiest garment in the world, but she was fairly sure that Mace would get the right idea about her intentions.

"Lie beside me," she said. "Hold me."

Though his dark eyes questioned, he did as she requested. His long body stretched out beside her. He was on top of the covers; she was beneath. His muscular arm stretched across her body, and he snuggled her against him with her head resting below his chin.

She inhaled his scent as she rubbed her cheek against his bare chest. With her fingertips she lightly caressed his flesh in widening circles, feeling the muscle beneath the skin and the outline of his rib cage. She found the nub of his nipple.

"Nicole." His voice was a low, soothing rumble. "Are you aware of what you're doing?"

"Oh, yes." She inched up until her face was right next to his. "You've been good to me, Mace. I want to make you happy."

Teasingly she kissed his chin. She nipped lightly at his mouth, caught his lower lip between her teeth and tugged.

His body moved against her. His leg straddled her thigh. Though there were several layers of material between them, she knew he was sexually excited.

Yet, when she tried to kiss him, he dodged. His voice was husky. "You don't owe me anything."

"Of course I do. You've taken care of me, given me a place to stay, fed me."

When she looked into his eyes, she could see how much he desired her. His gaze was blazing hot.

She whispered, "This is the least I can do to pay you back."

His voice sounded strangled. "No."

"Don't you want to make love to me?"

"More than anything in the world." But he pushed himself away until he was sitting on the edge of her bed. "But not like this. Not because you're paying off a debt."

She didn't understand. All men wanted to make love all the time. That was the way of the world. "Do you find me unattractive?"

"Nicole, you're an angel, the most beautiful woman I've ever known. I have dreams about your hair, tangling my fingers in your long golden hair."

"Then kiss me."

He gently placed his finger across her lips, silencing her. "I want more than your body, Nicole. Someday, when I make love to you, you'll be ready to give me your heart."

He leaned down and kissed her forehead. Then he rose from her bed and left the room.

She lay very still in the dim light of the bedside lamp. No man had ever refused her before. No man had ever asked for so much. He wanted more than just sex. He wanted her heart.

Love. The mere whisper of the word struck a chord in her heart, the first note to a crashing symphony. Was it possible to love him?

She rolled over on the bed and buried her face in the pillow. Could she ever give her heart away?

Her cheeks were damp. Her tears had begun to flow. She felt the floodgates burst. Years of suppressed emotions spilled from her. She cried for the loss of her parents, the loss of her innocence. Cleansing tears—all the tears she refused to shed when she'd been abused—poured from her. No holding back, she wept until her eyes ached, until the well was dry, until she fell asleep.

At last her dreams were peaceful and sweet.

Chapter Ten

The next morning Mace sat at the kitchen table, staring into his coffee mug. He'd pretty much decided that he was a pathetic excuse for a man. He'd turned down sex with a goddess. What the hell had he been thinking? It wasn't as if he'd ever considered himself to be a sensitive guy. And when it came to women, he never got it. He never figured out the right thing to say or the right gift. When relationships fell apart, including his marriage, he didn't have a clue about what he'd done wrong.

Last night it seemed as though he'd done the right thing with Nicole. Which didn't include jumping her bones. Damn it.

"You're grumpy this morning," Jewel said. "What's the problem, big brother?"

He wasn't about to share last night with his smart-aleck sister. "I've got stuff on my mind. A kidnapping. Ransom. A pea-brain special agent from the FBI."

"What do you think of Nicole?"

He looked up sharply. "What do you mean?"

She glanced up from the griddle with a taunting gleam in her eyes. "You like her."

"Yeah, she's okay."

"Ooh, Mace has a girlfriend." She smirked. "Weren't you even going to invite me to the wedding?"

"What wedding?"

"The one Daisy is catering."

The rumor from Las Ranas had already spread this far. Now he was stuck with jokes from his sister and probably from the rest of the local community. "Drop it, okay?"

"Seriously, Mace. I like Nicole. You could do a lot worse."

He rose from the table. "I'm out of here."

"Sit down, you big dope." She set a plate of hot cakes and bacon in front of him. "You need to eat something before you take on the FBI."

The breakfast smelled great. His hunger warred with his pride. Hunger won. He sat back down and started eating.

When Nicole entered the kitchen, he was aware of a change in the atmosphere. A brightness. A special warmth. What was it about her? In just a few days together, she'd grown on him. He wanted to know her better, to know the secrets of her heart.

"Smells fantastic," she said. "Sorry I'm too late to help with breakfast, Jewel."

"You're not too late to eat. Sit down."

When she took her place at the end of the table, Mace gazed into her face. In spite of a little puffiness around her eyes, she looked fresh and pretty, as if she had slept peacefully. Her hair was neatly braided, back in control. She offered him a wary smile that didn't reach her eyes. "Good morning, Mace."

"You're dressed," he said.

"Why wouldn't I be?"

"You could have slept in this morning," he said. "There's no need for you to come with me to the cabin. I meant what I said last night. It isn't your job to deal with the kidnappers."

"I'm going with you."

He'd prefer for her to stay here, safe and well protected by his deputies. "Why?"

"I remembered some advice from my mother," she said solemnly. "Joey helped me when I didn't have anywhere else to turn. I'll do the same for him."

He bit his tongue to keep from arguing with her and telling her that Joey was probably part of the kidnapping scheme and didn't deserve her loyalty. Nicole's mind was made up, and Mace had to respect her decision. "We're leaving in half an hour."

Jewel placed Nicole's plate in front of her and sat down. "Now," she said, "tell me about this wedding that Daisy is going to cater."

He groaned. It was going to be a very long and troublesome day.

THE FIRST THING Mace noticed when they arrived at the Wentworth cabin was that Special Agent Heflin had lost some of his spit and polish. He hadn't shaved. His jeans and turtleneck looked as if he'd slept in them. And he was muttering about not being able to get a decent cup of coffee.

"There's a coffee machine in the kitchen," Nicole said. "Why don't I make a fresh pot?"

"Yes," Heflin said. "That would be useful."

The two other agents trailed her into the kitchen while Heflin squared off with Mace. "I've thought it over. I can't accede to the kidnapper's demands. Nicole can't talk to them.''

"Fine with me," Mace said. "Have you considered the consequences?''

"That they'll kill the victim?" Heflin nodded. "I've thought of that. But if I give them the upper hand, I've got no leverage for negotiations.''

Mace didn't envy his position. Nor did he accept Heflin's reasoning. This situation was largely nonnegotiable, and Heflin was making it more complicated than necessary. "I don't think Joey would agree with you.''

"There's no guarantee he'll be safe whether the ransom is paid or not.''

There was the complicated piece. If Joey was, in fact, an innocent who was not part of the scheme, the kidnappers faced a great risk in releasing him because he could identify them. "When I saw them on the road, they wore ski masks," Mace said. "Maybe they've kept him blindfolded.''

"He's an artist," Heflin reminded. "He's trained to remember visual details.''

"You can't write him off. We should do what the kidnappers instruct.''

"I want to control the delivery of the ransom so we know Joey is safe when the money is in the kidnappers' hands.''

"Like a hostage exchange," Mace said.

"Exactly.''

"What kind of surveillance have you got in place?''

"There's a chopper standing by at the airport. We have chase teams ready to roll.''

The door to the cabin flew open, and a gray-haired

man in an expensive camel-hair overcoat strode inside. "Blake Wentworth."

He announced his name as though they should be impressed. Behind him, he pulled a large, square, canvas suitcase on wheels. "I've got the ransom."

After Heflin and Mace introduced themselves, Wentworth said, "Where's the girl?"

Nicole came out of the kitchen. Mace smiled to himself when he noticed that she had resumed the princess attitude she used to disguise her inner turmoil. He could almost imagine the tiara when she presented herself. "Hello, Mr. Wentworth. I'm so pleased to meet you."

"The girl in the painting," he said. "You're very attractive, dear. I understand why my nephew has scheduled so many trips to Elkhorn."

"Joey and I are friends, nothing more."

"Come on, Nicole." Blake grimaced. "I think we all know why you and Joey are living together. You're after his inheritance, aren't you?"

She didn't react, but Mace did. He wanted to punch this hotshot businessman in his pearly-white teeth. "Back off, Blake."

His steely-eyed gaze transferred from Nicole to Mace. "Excuse me?"

"There's no need to insult the lady," Mace said. "If you don't mind, we have important issues to discuss before the kidnappers call."

"Such as?" His irritation was evident; Blake didn't like being called down by a small-town sheriff. "We pay the ransom. Joey is returned. Simple."

"Not quite," Heflin said.

While he explained the kidnapper's demands and his own reluctance to follow them, Blake continued to glare at Mace. They sized each other up, measuring strengths and weaknesses. Physically, Mace was far superior, but Uncle Blake had money and power as the CEO of Wentworth Oil Exploration, an international company. Big deal! All the wealth in the world didn't compensate for Blake's impoverished spirit. By attacking Nicole, he showed the baseness of his character.

"...and so," Heflin concluded, "I should be the one to take the phone call."

"Don't be an ass," Blake said. "We'll do *exactly* as the kidnappers demand. Nicole takes the call and follows their instructions."

Heflin objected, "With all due respect—"

"My nephew Joey might be a waste of skin, but he's still my nephew, and I want him returned safely. We do it my way."

"This is my jurisdiction," Heflin said. "This operation will run according to FBI procedure."

"Fine. As long as that procedure is to follow the kidnappers' instructions." Blake loosened the buttons on his expensive camel coat. "Wentworth Oil Exploration operates in third-world countries where kidnappings with ransom demands sometimes happen. I've found that it's best to do what the kidnappers say."

"Not according to my information," Heflin said.

"It's my money," Blake said. "I'm calling the shots."

Mace edged out of the discussion and stood beside Nicole. "Are you okay?"

"I can handle this," she said quietly. "Actually, I hate that I'm on the same side as Blake."

The phone rang.

The room went silent.

"Go ahead," Mace said to Nicole. "Pick it up."

As she lifted the receiver, the other two agents hurried to monitor their electronic stations. One of them whispered, "Keep them on the line as long as possible."

"Hello," she said. Her voice was broadcast over a speaker phone that allowed everyone in the room to hear both sides of the conversation.

"Hello, Nicole." The voice sounded distorted, mechanically altered. It wasn't Joey. "Do you have the ransom?"

"Yes," she said, mindful that she should stretch out the conversation. "I think it's all here, but I should probably—"

"Take the money and go to Joey's car. You'll find a cell phone in the glove compartment. We'll give you instructions on the phone."

"Could you repeat that?" she asked.

"If anyone follows you, Joey's dead. If you're wearing a bug, Joey's dead. No helicopters. No electronic surveillance."

"I'm not sure what you mean." She tried to play for time. "Please repeat everything."

"Go now."

The phone call ended abruptly.

Heflin stood behind one of the other agents who was wearing headphones. "Did you get a trace?"

"Sorry," the other agent said. "It's the same cell phone. They're in this area, but I can't pinpoint the location."

"Let's get going," Blake said. "You heard them."

"Not so fast," Helfin said. "We have surveillance possibilities to consider."

As the men discussed, Nicole sat trembling, afraid

that she'd made the wrong decision about delivering the ransom herself. *Joey's dead.* The voice on the phone repeated those words twice. If she made a mistake, Joey would be killed. And what about the danger to her?

Fear crept through her, distorting her perceptions. Under threat of violence, she didn't behave rationally. All she knew how to do was duck and run.

Mace rested his hand on her shoulder. "Don't worry. I'm coming with you."

A wave of relief washed over her. She almost collapsed in his arms. Then she remembered. "You can't come with me. They said no surveillance."

"They didn't say you had to be alone in the car." He turned to Heflin. "I'm assuming you've swept the area for bugs and surveillance cameras. The kidnappers aren't watching the cabin."

"I guarantee they aren't." Heflin said. "I have men posted outside. The kidnappers might be able to watch the road, but they can't see this cabin."

"I'm going with Nicole," Mace said. "I'll lie down in the back seat so they can't see me."

Uncle Blake confronted him. "Don't try to be a hero, Sheriff."

"I don't have to try, sir. It comes naturally."

Nicole cracked a small smile. Mace was right about being a natural hero. The rest of these men were cracking under the pressure. Only Mace stayed cool and controlled. He *was* a hero, her hero. He would keep her safe. She said, "Gentlemen, I won't go through with this unless Mace is with me."

"Fine," Heflin said. He gave a small phone to Mace. "This is what you use to communicate with me. Make sure Joey is safe before you release the money."

There was a flurry of activity. The wheeled suitcase filled with the ransom money was transported to the car while various arguments raged about whether or not to put tracking devices on the car.

Nicole didn't feel herself walking, but she was somehow behind the steering wheel of Joey's Beemer. She opened the glove compartment. The car keys were there as was a cell phone. It rang.

"Go ahead," Mace said from the back seat. "Answer it."

She pressed Talk and held the phone to her ear. "Hello."

The mechanical voice answered. "Drive to the first stop sign in Elkhorn, turn right at Elm Street. Stay on that road. I'll call again in fifteen minutes. Start the car now."

She disconnected the call and dropped the phone on the passenger seat. "Mace, I'm scared."

He stretched his arm between the bucket seats and clasped her hand. "You can do this. I'm right here to back you up. What did he say?"

She repeated the instructions. "I'm supposed to start the car now."

"Go ahead," Mace said. "Do it."

Driving carefully, she maneuvered around the several vehicles surrounding her formerly secluded cabin. Her fingers gripped the steering wheel. Every cell in her body screamed with tension.

From the back seat, Mace said, "You're doing fine."

"How do you know?" she snapped. "You're lying

down and can't see what I'm doing. For all you know, I might be driving down the wrong side of the road.''

When he laughed, a responding smile tightened her lips. She was so grateful that he was here.

He said, "I wish I had a spy periscope so I could see where you're going."

"Are there any special instructions I should be aware of?"

"Only one," he said. "Make sure Joey is safe before you turn over the ransom. Once they've got the money, there's no reason to keep him alive. Ask to talk to him."

When she pulled up to the first stop sign, she could see the Elkhorn Café farther down the block. On a normal day, she might be there, working the morning shift so the owner, Deborah, could have some time off. Though waitressing wasn't what she'd call a terrific career choice, she longed to go back there. Her former life had been so calm. She wished that none of this had ever happened.

But if Joey had never been kidnapped, she'd never have gotten to know Mace. Now they were close. In her mind they were more intimate than if they'd made love. She hadn't really had time to process what happened last night, but she knew he'd given her a precious gift. His respect.

"Where are we now?" he asked.

"Driving west on Elm Street, almost beyond the houses. Has it been fifteen minutes yet?"

"Almost," he said.

"I'm glad you're here, Mace. If I was doing this myself, I'd be scared to death."

"Don't get too happy," he said. "You need to stay alert."

"No problem." She mentally measured her stress level. "I'm still incredibly tense."

"You'll be okay. There's no reason for the kidnappers to hurt you."

She prayed he was right.

The cell phone rang, and she pulled over to the side of the road before she answered.

The instructions were terse, but she noticed right away that the mechanically altered voice had changed to normal tones. "Turn right at Route 188. I'll call back in another fifteen minutes."

She relayed the information to Mace who passed it on through his cell phone. At Route 188, she turned right through fields that lay cold and fallow in October. This area was populated only by the occasional farmhouse, several of which looked deserted. She shuddered, hoping she wouldn't be asked to walk into a deserted house to drop off the ransom.

Another scary thought occurred to her. "Mace, you won't be able to come with me when I leave the car with the ransom."

"I'm thinking about that," he said. "The kidnappers were clear about the fact that you shouldn't wear a bug. But you've got a cell phone and so do I. Before you leave the car, call my number and leave the connection open so I can hear what's going on."

She doubted he'd be able to hear much if the phone was in her pocket, but it was better than nothing. "That makes me feel a little safer."

"If you want, I can take the phone. They'll be stuck dealing with me."

She considered for a moment. Though she'd love to be free from this responsibility, the kidnappers had been clear. If she failed to follow their instructions, they would kill Joey. "I won't risk it. If Joey gets killed because I was too scared to answer a telephone, I couldn't live with myself."

"I'm here for backup," he said. "Stay calm."

Calm? That couldn't be further from the way she felt. Her pulse rate throbbed in triple time. Nervous sweat made her feel clammy under her parka.

Mace asked, "How fast are you going?"

Nicole checked the speedometer. She was driving nearly twenty miles per hour over the limit. Joey's Beemer provided a very smooth ride. On the long stretches of straight road, it was easy to speed.

Her foot lifted from the accelerator pedal. "How did you know I was speeding?"

"I'm a cop," he said. "Speed limits are my bread and butter."

She chuckled with surprising relief. "Are you telling me that cops stop speeders just to collect the fines?"

"Yeah, sure." His sarcastic tone rose from the back seat. "Most days, I've got nothing better to do than lurk around behind bushes at the side of the road, waiting to nab unsuspecting tourists."

She grinned, unable to imagine Mace doing anything so petty. He was bigger than that—larger than life. Not only was he efficient, but everybody in the county knew who he was, and they respected him. "You might not be tracking down notorious criminals every day of the week, but I'll bet the reason there's order in Sterling County is because you're here."

"I like the way you think."

"Is that all you like about me?" She regretted the words as soon as they slipped out. Now was not the time for a relationship discussion. And yet she truly wanted to know if she was special to him. Last night he said he wanted to know her heart.

"I shouldn't tell you this," he said. "But I get a kick out of your sassy comments. I like the way you act tough."

"Me? I'm a huge scaredy-cat."

"You're no pussy cat," he said. "You're a cougar. Lean and tawny, scratching a livelihood from the desert plains. You've had to fight to survive."

His description made her feel braver. If she'd had someone like Mace at her side, she might have followed a more productive path, might have been worthy of respect. But she'd made so many mistakes, so many foolish decisions.

He said, "I believe in you, Nicole."

She wanted to turn around and kiss him. "I trust you, too. A hundred percent."

"You trust me?"

"Sure."

That wasn't true, and he knew she was holding back.

"Are we coming to a town?" he asked.

Beside the road she saw a sign. "Ellensburg."

"Tell me what you see."

"It's tiny. A gas station and a general store."

"Do you see a dark-colored Jeep?" he asked. "Anybody sitting in a parked car?"

She described two men at the gas station, talking. "They're both wearing baseball caps, jeans and jackets."

The phone rang again.

From the back seat, Mace reminded, "Ask for Joey. Tell them they don't get the money until you talk to Joey."

She pressed Talk.

The mechanical-sounding voice on the phone said, "Stop at the general store in Ellensburg."

"I've already driven past it," she said. "And I won't do anything else until I talk to Joey. I need to know he's all right."

"Turn around and go back to the general store in Ellensburg."

"I mean it." Her voice quavered. "I have to talk to Joey first."

"Hang on, bitch."

Dead air came across the phone line.

She swerved to the side of the road and slammed the car into Park. Apprehension gathered like dark clouds before a cloudburst, but she had to stand up to her fear and be clear in her demands. If she didn't talk to Joey before the kidnappers had the ransom, they could kill him.

"Nicole?"

"Joey! You're okay."

"Listen, you've got to do what these guys tell you to do. Understand?"

"Not until I'm sure you're safe. Tell them! Tell them I have to hear from your own lips that you're safe before I'll deliver the money."

"Okay," he said. "I'll tell them. Just don't screw this up."

"Be careful, Joey. I don't want anything bad to happen to you."

"Too late." He chuckled. She couldn't believe that he was laughing while she was gripped by fear. The inside of her head pounded.

She turned in the seat to look back at Mace. His dark eyes reassured her. He reached toward her, and she gripped his hand. Thank God he was here! If she'd been alone, Nicole never would have thought to negotiate.

The other voice returned. "You'll know Joey is safe before the final delivery."

"Good," she said.

"Now, go back to Ellensburg. Take the ransom from the car. Go inside and buy a pack of cigarettes."

"I don't smoke," Nicole said.

"Are you always this dumb or are you trying to tick me off?"

She immediately recognized the tone. He was a bully, an abuser. He might have been her stepfather. Or Derek. And she knew better than to fight him. She cowered, waiting for the pain that she knew would come. "I'm sorry. So sorry."

"Do what I say. Go to the general store. Take the cell phone with you. I might call while you're inside. Go now."

He disconnected.

She tossed the cell phone onto the passenger seat, wishing she could throw it through a window, start up the car and drive into another dimension.

Mace still held her other hand. "What did he say? Tell me quick."

Wobbling at the verge of a scream, she relayed the conversation. "And I should go now."

He pulled her hand to his lips and kissed her fingertips. "You did well. Nobody, not even Heflin could have done better. Let's get moving."

She started up the car and pulled a U-turn. "Since I have to keep the cell phone line open for the kidnappers, I can't stay in touch with you."

"If it comes to a confrontation, drop the money

and run. I'll watch for you. I won't let these guys get away.''

''Not until we know Joey's safe,'' she said.

''Right,'' he said. ''Be careful, Nicole.''

She parked in front of the general store, got the wheeled suitcase from the trunk and walked inside, pulling eight hundred thousand dollars in cash behind her.

Chapter Eleven

Mace crouched in the back of the BMW sedan with his automatic pistol in his fist. Frustrated by his inability to act, he felt his muscles coil into tight knots. He hated waiting, but he couldn't leave the car because the kidnappers might be watching the vehicle. Likely, they were observing. Likely, this stop in Ellensburg was a test to make sure Nicole wasn't accompanied by a horde of Feds.

He called Heflin on the cell phone and whispered their location. "Do not," Mace said, "I repeat, do not approach."

"Is this the drop?"

"Doubtful," Mace said. "They promised proof of Joey's safety before we turn over the cash."

"Keep us apprised."

"Roger." Mace disconnected.

Through the slightly opened window of the Beemer, he listened intently for any sound indicating Nicole might be in trouble. He was worried about her. She was scared to death, literally quaking with fear. It took a lot of courage on her part to walk into that general store alone, and he wasn't sure how long her strength would last.

He wanted to be at her side, protecting her instead of hiding. Remembering the lessons he learned when hunting with Tata Charlie, Mace told himself to be patient, to wait until his quarry came into view, wait for the perfect moment to attack. The pent-up need for action must not overrule a hunter's wisdom.

He concentrated on figuring out the mind of the kidnappers. From what Nicole reported of their last communication, he deduced they hadn't been watching the road. Otherwise, they'd have known when she drove too far, passing through Ellensburg. So where were they? Why did they want her to come inside the store?

One reason might be that they wanted to lay down a pattern of obedience from Nicole, wearing down her resistance. Or they might want to get a look at the suitcase holding the money, to gauge the size and figure out how they were going to grab it. The worst possible scenario? They meant to take the ransom now.

Mace doubted that plan. Ellensburg was in the middle of wide-open spaces and few roads. Escape from here without being noticed would be almost impossible. Better escape routes were near the foothills where rutted roads and pathways led through a labyrinth of mesas, arroyos and canyons.

Or they could wait until dark. He winced when he thought of that possibility. Spending the entire day in the back of the Beemer would be difficult for him. And it would be hell for Nicole. Her nerves were already stretched to the limit.

He heard the trunk of the Beemer open. There was a scuffing noise as the suitcase was lifted inside and the lid slammed. Nicole was back in the front seat.

"They called while I was inside," she said as she started the car. "I'm supposed to stay on this route until they call again in fifteen minutes."

Mace glimpsed the nape of her neck and the edge of her jaw. He saw her delicate white fingers curl around the steering wheel. When she turned to look through the rear window to back out of the parking space, she glanced at him. Her blue eyes seemed murky and dulled as if she was losing strength.

"Are you okay?" he asked.

"I feel kind of numb." A tremulous smile fell from her lips. "There's only so long a person can be terrified before…"

"Before what?"

"Before you accept your fate, no matter how awful."

He understood what she was saying. After a physical injury, the body goes into shock to deaden the senses and ease the pain. It was the same with intense emotions. Sooner or later adrenaline was spent. Fear could not be sustained forever. "Don't give up."

She drove for a while without speaking. From his position in the back seat, all he could see was a sky filled with gathering storm clouds. Yesterday had been sunny, and it was still too warm for snow.

"Rain," he said aloud. "They're waiting for the rain."

"What?"

"If we get a downpour, the FBI chopper won't be as useful for surveillance."

"I don't understand," she said.

"They planned the ransom delivery for today when it would rain." But that couldn't be right. They had to wait for Blake Wentworth to arrive with the ransom money. That was the real reason they couldn't schedule anything for yesterday. "Forget I said that. Nobody can predict the Colorado weather."

The cell phone rang again, and Nicole answered.

It drove Mace crazy to hear only her side of the conversation. He was certain that there were clues in what the kidnappers said.

She dropped the phone quickly. "I'm supposed to turn right at the next town. It seems like I'm making a circle."

"Headed back toward the foothills," he said. Using his cell phone, he relayed the information to Heflin.

After she made the turn, Nicole said, "There's something I need to tell you, Mace."

"Shoot," he said.

"A little while ago, I was talking about trust. Between you and me."

His jaw clenched. Relationship talks were never his favorite thing. En route to a ransom drop, he definitely didn't want to open this bag of worms. "Maybe we should discuss this at another time."

"I want to do it now. It's best if I don't have to face you."

"While I'm stuck in the back seat of a Beemer." With no way out, he had to listen. "What is it, Nicole?"

"We both know I haven't been completely honest with you."

There was a catch in her voice. He knew how hard it must be for her to tell him these closely guarded secrets. "Go on," he said.

"I moved in with Joey because I'm on the run."

"From what?"

"Before I came to Elkhorn, I was married for four months."

Married? That one came out of the blue. "Your marriage didn't show up on any record checks."

"I never legally changed my name. Maybe somewhere in the back of my mind, I knew the marriage wasn't going to work."

It was an incredibly simple ploy, especially for a woman like Nicole who had no family and refused to tell the name of the few friends who might make the connection. Still, her deception didn't answer any of the important questions. Why had she married? Who was this man? Why the hell had she kept her marriage a secret?

"He was wealthy," she said. "The life he offered me was something I could only dream about. Designer clothes. Magnificent jewelry. A mansion fit for a princess."

She had married for money. He didn't like the idea, but he understood the appeal. "This very wealthy man. Why did he marry you?"

"Because I was pretty and young." She made those attributes sound like a curse. "I was his trophy wife."

Mace didn't need to see her face to know the depth of her regret. He heard guilt and shame in her voice. She knew that she'd made a bad decision.

She continued, "It was my job to look good on his arm, to make all the other men jealous. I never left the house without complete makeup and perfect style. Derek made sure I always looked good. If he noticed anything wrong—a lipstick that was too dark or a hemline that was too long—he made me go back to my bedroom and start over until I got it right. I learned to hate those designer clothes.''

Which explained why she never bothered with lipstick or styling her hair anymore. "What happened next?"

"Since I was only a possession, he didn't even pretend to respect me. The verbal abuse started on the honeymoon. Then the beatings.''

The heat of anger surged through Mace's veins. Men who hurt women disgusted him. "Why didn't you tell the police?"

"Did I mention that Derek was a high-powered lawyer? And I was nothing. Eye candy. A bimbo. Nobody would've listened to me. And Derek would've punished me for embarrassing him. So I ran away.'' She was talking faster, as though anxious to finish her story. "And I couldn't tell you or Agent Heflin because you'd contact Derek. Then he'd know where I was, and he'd come after me.''

His anger turned to outrage, and it burned in his gut. Her story sparked his instinctual hatred for injustice.

Her admission shouldn't have been a complete surprise to him. He knew her childhood included abuse from her stepfather, and it was an unfortunate fact that people who had been treated badly often fell into similar relationships with a spouse. But Nicole was more than a statistic to him. He cared for her on a deep, almost cellular level that he didn't completely understand. He admired her innate beauty and her sharp intelligence. She was a real woman with many dimensions, and she had survived against all odds.

It almost felt as if he was born to be her protector, that he'd spent his life waiting for her. The fact that she'd been another man's wife, his plaything, was hard to accept.

"Can you forgive me?" she asked.

"You don't need my forgiveness. It's your life. You don't have to apologize for your decisions."

"Now that you know what I really am, you despise me."

"It's good that you told me about your past. I wouldn't have wanted to find out in another way."

Mace stared up at the ceiling of the car, looking for an answer that wasn't readily apparent. He wished he could take her into his arms to reassure her. But that would be too easy.

He didn't hate her. But could he still respect a woman who allowed herself to be used in such a way, who sold herself for luxury? Mace warred within himself. The Nicole he knew was not a shallow woman. She worked hard and didn't complain. "You did what you had to. You survived."

"Yes." The single word was a gasp.

"You can trust me," he said. "Your secrets are safe with me."

When the cell phone rang again, he was thrown back into a different reality. They were still on a chase to find the men who had abducted Joey Wentworth.

Now Mace could see why she was so devoted to Joey. He'd been her refuge. As she'd said before, she'd had nowhere else to turn.

She ended the call quickly. "I'm supposed to make another turn to the north."

Mace raised his head to take a quick peek at the surrounding landscape. The lowering clouds threatened a downpour. "We'll be headed toward Yellow Creek. That's a bigger town with more traffic. And it's near the foothills. We might be approaching the drop.''

''What should I do?''

''Be sure Joey is safe before you agree to stop. Demand to talk to him on the phone just like you did the last time.''

''It's starting to rain,'' she said as she turned on the windshield wipers. ''Do you really think this might be the place?''

''It's possible.''

Only a moment later the phone rang again, and she grabbed it. Now that she'd told Mace her story, she was doubly anxious for this to be over. She wanted to see his face, to read his expression and discover how he really felt about her. ''Hello?''

''In Yellow Creek,'' the gruff voice said, ''park at the convenience store on Main and Caliente. Go inside. Bring the ransom and the cell phone.''

''Not until I hear from Joey,'' she said.

''He'll call you.''

''If I don't know for sure that he's safe, I won't bring the—''

''He'll call.''

She glared at the dead phone in her hand. Though the danger had not abated one whit, she felt more anger than fear. All this racing around the countryside was a deliberate plan to throw her off-kilter. But she wouldn't give in, wouldn't lose control. Her entire life was a practice drill for this very situation. She hadn't fallen apart when her father had passed away, or at her mother's deathbed. When her stepfather had abused her and when Derek had continued the pattern, she hadn't wept. She could do this!

''Nicole?''

"I'm all right," she said firmly. Even telling Mace about her marriage to Derek seemed like a relief. Now it was done. If he'd lost his respect for her, so be it. She informed him, "I'm supposed to stop at the convenience store in Yellow Creek. This is another time when I take the ransom when I go inside."

"I'll let Heflin know."

Nicole realized that she was already approaching the town. She was on Main Street. After all these long waits between phone calls, the pace had suddenly picked up. Everything was moving too fast.

She squinted through the steadily falling rain, trying to read street signs. She saw what she was looking for. Caliente Street. When she parked at the convenience store, the phone rang again.

"It's me." Joey's voice sounded lighter than before, almost happy. "I'm okay. I'm safe."

"Are you sure?"

"Listen carefully, Nicole. They said I could only talk for two minutes."

"Okay."

"You're the one in danger now. If you don't do what they say, they'll kill you. And they mean it."

She couldn't quite comprehend the shift in focus. Her fear had been centered on Joey.

"I'm okay," he said. "They shoved me out of the car and drove off. I don't know where I am, but there's a town up ahead."

"You're going that way?"

"I'll be there in a sec. I'm totally fine," he said. "I've got to get off the phone. Do what they say. Be careful."

She disconnected. Before she had a chance to report to Mace, the phone rang again. The kidnapper said, "We know there's someone else in your car."

How could they know? She glanced through the downpour at the parking lot. There was no one else in sight. Sometime during this roundabout journey to hell and back, the kidnappers must have been watching.

"Say nothing to him," the kidnapper instructed. "Or you both will die. Do you understand?"

"Yes."

"Go inside now. Bring the suitcase."

The fear she thought she'd left behind was back in full force. Joey was no longer in danger but she was. And so was Mace. Too easily, she imagined high-powered rifles trained upon them. A sniper could be hiding in the trees beside the store. A fast car could swoop up beside them.

"Nicole," Mace said from the back seat. "What's going on? Why did the phone ring twice."

Her lips pressed tightly together. If she told him what was going on, she might be signing their death warrants.

"Nicole?"

"I'll explain when I get back."

She left the BMW and went to the trunk. Removing the heavy black canvas suitcase was more of a struggle this time. Rain splattered on her head and shoulders. She felt helpless and clumsy, unable to think ahead. Her only goal was to follow the instructions exactly.

The inside of the convenience store was similar to thousands of other stores with well-stocked rows of products in small, overpriced containers. The clerk behind the counter, a teenage boy in a blue uniform jacket, called out, "Wet enough for you?"

"It's raining," she said vaguely.

"Something wrong, ma'am?"

"No, I'm fine." She dragged the suitcase down the aisle toward the cooler full of soda pop and beer.

The cell phone rang. The instruction was terse. "Go to the ladies' room."

In the far right corner of the store, behind a display rack of pantyhose, was a sign for the rest rooms. She stumbled toward it. Every step felt like a mistake. She wanted to turn around and run back to the car.

She pushed the door open. Two men in black ski masks stood inside the small room with a sink, a mirror and a stall. The taller man grabbed her arm roughly. "Don't make a sound."

The cold bore of a pistol pressed against her neck. She recoiled, then stiffened. Pain and abuse resonated in her memory. The wounds never truly healed. There was always an unassuageable ache—a scar that would never heal. She swallowed hard to keep from crying out.

The other man unzipped the suitcase. Moving quickly, he removed the bundled money, stuffed it into heavy-duty garbage bags.

The man who gripped her arm whispered into her ear. "You're real pretty, Nicole."

Revulsion crawled through her. She wanted to spit but knew better than to aggravate him. She'd been here before. The safest course was nonresistance.

"Here's what you're going to do next," he said. "You're going to take the suitcase and go back to the car. Understand?"

She nodded.

He tightened his grip on her arm. "Say it."

"I understand."

"Good," he said. "Don't tell the guy in the back seat that you turned over the ransom. Not until I call. Understand?"

"Yes."

"You keep driving like nothing happened."

His partner had removed all the money. He threw two heavy bundles of newspapers into the suitcase.

"Nicole," the tall guy whispered gruffly. "If you tell him, you're both going to die. You don't want that to happen, do you?"

"No."

He released her with a shove that sent her sprawling on the dirty tile floor. He grabbed one of the bags full of money. "Count to a hundred. Then leave."

They were gone. She stayed on the floor on her hands and knees. Shudders wracked her body. She had to regain control. If she said anything to Mace, they'd be killed. She didn't know how the kidnappers would make good on their threat, but she was certain they'd do it. There was no choice but to obey.

Slowly she gripped the edge of the sink and hauled herself off the floor. She washed her hands and stared in the mirror at her stricken face. Mace couldn't see her like this. He'd know something was wrong. She lifted her eyebrows and straightened the corners of her lips into a mask.

Pulling the suitcase behind her, she left the rest room. The kidnappers hadn't gone out this way, not with the clerk watching. They must have taken a back exit. Forcing her composure, she headed for the front door of the convenience store.

Outside, the rain sluiced down, pelting her head

and shoulders as she rounded the BMW. Struggling, she lifted the suitcase filled with newspapers into the trunk. Running around to the driver's side, she slipped behind the steering wheel.

"What happened?" Mace demanded. "Nicole, talk to me."

"Another false alarm." She hated lying to him. "Like at the other store."

"Why did you get two phone calls before you went inside?"

"The first one disconnected." She ran her hand over her hair, wiping away the rain. The windshield was fogged; she couldn't see out. But she needed to get away from here, to put distance between herself and a possible sniper.

She scrubbed at the windshield with her bare hand, making a hole where she could see. Turning the key in the ignition, she started the wipers and the defroster. "I'm supposed to drive again. Another call will come in fifteen minutes."

When she looked over her shoulder to back out, she saw him staring. His eyes accused her. "Something's wrong," he said.

She tore her gaze away. "I can't talk right now."

In reverse, she blindly swung around and drove out of the parking lot. She was on Main Street again, cruising through the town of Yellow Creek. Pelting rain obscured her vision. Though it was noon, the skies were dark and foreboding.

But Joey was safe. The ransom was delivered. In moments she could tell Mace the truth, and this would be all over.

On the outskirts of the town, he sat up in the back seat. His touch on her arm was exquisitely gentle.

"The kidnappers met you in that store. They took the ransom money."

She said nothing. Her silence was all that kept them safe.

"One of those calls before you went inside," he said. "It was Joey."

The truth wrenched from her. "They said I couldn't tell you. They knew you were in the car, and they said they'd kill both of us if I didn't do what they said."

"It's okay." He stroked the sodden length of her hair. "You did the right thing."

She wanted to pull over but didn't dare stop. They might be following. "I have to keep driving until they call."

"Where's Joey?"

"I don't know his location. He said that he was fine. The kidnappers dropped him off outside a town and he was walking toward it."

"I'm going to call Heflin and fill him in. You keep driving."

She concentrated on the road, barely hearing Mace's conversation. The weight of the past days should have lifted from her shoulders, but she still felt burdened. Until she finally saw Joey face-to-face, she would worry.

The cell phone rang again. She hoped this would be the last time.

"Nicole." She recognized the voice of the tall man in the black ski mask. "No more instructions for now."

"I hope they catch you," she said. "I hope you go to prison."

He laughed. "Until we meet again."

"What do you mean? Don't hang up."

But the call disconnected, and she was left holding the phone, still uncertain. She drove onto the shoulder of the road and cut the engine. The danger hadn't passed. Not yet.

Her self-control was crumbling. How long could she withstand this pressure? Turning in the driver's seat, she looked back at Mace, who was still on the phone, giving precise location information to Heflin.

"We'll need a door-to-door search in Yellow River," he said. "They might be holed up."

His gaze fixed on Nicole, he reached toward her.

It was the only signal she needed. Nicole climbed between the bucket seats. In the back with Mace, she flung her arms around his neck and snuggled against him, needing his strong, solid reassurance.

He stroked her shoulders while continuing to talk on the cell phone. "My deputies can handle the search. People around here might be more willing to talk with them."

She turned off her brain, wanting only to be held. The warmth of his body soothed her.

"No," he said. "I don't know Joey's precise location. He has a cell phone. He ought to be smart enough to call 9-1-1."

After a pause he turned off the cell phone.

He embraced her for a good, long time, and it felt as if he was holding back the danger. While she was in his arms, nothing bad would happen.

Gently he released the tension in his arms. He tilted back her head to peer into her eyes, and she saw a thousand unspoken questions in his gaze. But he didn't say a word.

His mouth claimed hers. Though she hadn't expected his kiss, she returned his passion. Relief flooded through her. So much had passed between them without being able to touch, to express their closeness.

His tongue penetrated her lips, and she felt the awakening of desire. Pure sensation flowed between them. She wanted him with an intensity she'd never felt before. With Mace, she would not hold back. There would be openness between them. No lies. No fear.

Chapter Twelve

Back at the Wentworth cabin, after several hours of watching the misbegotten investigation under the FBI's jurisdiction, Mace drew three conclusions: Special Agent Heflin was a hopeless jackass; Blake Wentworth had a heart of stone; and Nicole was the closest thing anybody had to a suspect.

"Let's go over this again," Heflin said to her for what had to be the ten-thousandth time.

"Not again," Blake Wentworth groaned. "We've heard her story. Find another witness."

"There are no other witnesses," Heflin said. "Except for Mace."

"Oh, yes," Blake said with a sneer. "Our hero, Sheriff Mace. We know where he was while my money was being stolen. Our hero was hiding in the back of the car."

"Don't start with me," Mace warned. He was at the ragged end of self-restraint. He'd like nothing better than to squash Blake Wentworth like the money-grubbing cockroach he was. Blake hadn't shed a tear for Joey; his only concern was the ransom.

"Or what?"

Aiming a hard, steady gaze at the gray-haired Denver businessman, Mace kept his tone calm and businesslike. "I won't take bull from you, sir."

Blake scoffed, but he sank back on the beat-up sofa and closed his mouth. His arms folded across his chest, creasing his cashmere sweater.

Heflin cleared his throat and returned his attention to Nicole. "What did Joey say to you on the phone?"

Her poise was wearing thin. Though her posture was ramrod straight as she sat in the rocking chair, her complexion was wan. Exhaustion etched fine lines around her mouth and eyes.

Mace could hardly believe she was the same woman who cuddled warmly in his lap and returned his kisses with a heat that could only be described as pure passion. He yearned to hold her again, to savor the moment when she came alive in his arms. Though their time together could be measured in hours, he felt as if he'd been waiting an eternity for her. Later, he thought, as he rubbed his hand across his eyes. Tonight, he thought, tonight he would make love to her.

But right now his top priority was to get her away from Heflin and this pointless interrogation. She needed sleep and a good meal.

In a tired voice, she answered Heflin's question, "Joey told me he was okay. He'd been released and was walking toward a town."

"What town?"

"I don't know."

"That was five hours ago," Heflin said. "We still haven't heard from Joey."

"I know," she said quietly.

The fact that Joey had not yet shown up was strike

one against her. Nobody had spoken to him except Nicole.

Strike two was that she'd turned over the ransom without informing Mace or Heflin.

Her decision made sense to Mace. She hadn't said anything because she was terrified, afraid for her life. But Heflin interpreted her cooperation differently. He thought she'd conspired with the kidnappers, had purposely misled everyone, had helped the kidnappers get away clean—leaving not a trace behind.

Thus far Heflin's investigative strategy had been to put a chopper in the air as soon as the rain cleared, and to have his FBI agents fan out across the county. The Feds were questioning everybody, throwing their weight around and generally making the residents of Sterling County uncomfortable.

Mace had told him that his approach wouldn't work. Folks in these parts were independent, self-sufficient and generally suspicious of strangers. It wasn't that Sterling County residents were unfriendly, but they didn't like being pushed around and weren't likely to cooperate with the men in black.

But Heflin didn't listen, didn't care. This was his jurisdiction and he was going to direct operations according to procedure—no matter how misguided.

"It's getting late," Mace said. "I should take Nicole back to my ranch house and let her get some rest."

"I want her here," Heflin said.

"There's nothing more she can do."

Heflin paced nervously in the small cabin like a pit bull on a short leash. "There's something she hasn't told me yet."

"Believe me," Nicole said coldly. "I want this to be over as much as you do."

"Where's Joey?"

"I don't know," she snapped. "You're supposed to be the special agent. Solve this mess."

"Who are you protecting?"

She rolled her eyes. "Nobody."

"You're in the center of everything. You could have planned this whole scheme," Heflin accused. "I wouldn't be surprised to find out that you're the mastermind."

"That's me, all right. A master criminal. I'm Al Capone and Ma Barker and Bonnie and Clyde all rolled into one."

"Enough," Blake Wentworth said. "I've heard enough of this petty squabbling."

"Sir," Heflin said, "with all due respect, I—"

"The bottom line," Blake interrupted, "is that I paid top dollar for my nephew's safety and he hasn't been returned. I've been gypped."

Mace felt his lip curl in disgust. With this guy, it was always about the money.

Blake rose from the sofa and announced, "I'm leaving. I'll be at the Elkhorn Inn."

Heflin breathed an almost audible sigh of relief. "That's probably for the best, sir. We'll keep you informed."

"I don't want minute-by-minute updates." He thrust his arms into his camel overcoat. "I want results."

"Yes, sir."

"Contact me when you have news about my nephew."

As Blake strode toward the door, Mace permitted

himself a wry smile. He was fairly sure that the accommodations in Libby Tynsdale's boarding house were a lot less luxurious than Blake expected.

Heflin sank into a chair beside the table where the state-of-the-art FBI surveillance equipment was arrayed. None of his electronics nor the helicopter search had produced results. His investigation was going nowhere fast. Under his breath he muttered, "Blake Wentworth is going to get me in a lot of trouble."

Mace sympathized. "A rich guy like him must have powerful friends and influence."

"He's not as big a hotshot as he thinks," Heflin said. "We've looked into his company finances. He's hurting. He couldn't have come up with that ransom on his own."

"Not many people could," Mace said. But most people who were on a budget didn't parade around in thousand-dollar overcoats. No doubt it took a lot of capital to run Blake's multinational empire.

"If my career wasn't on the line," Heflin said, "I wouldn't mind seeing Blake lose his money."

For the first time, Heflin had dropped his guard and was exchanging confidences like a regular cop. Mace hoped this signaled a change in attitude. He offered, "If you want, I can take over the investigation from here."

"How? You've already got most of your deputies posted at roadblocks."

"Here's the thing," Mace said. "The roadblocks were your idea. And I've got to tell you, they aren't real effective. For one thing, you can see the road-block from a long way off and turn around. For another, there are too many back roads and byways to catch every vehicle.''

"Don't care," Heflin said. "The roadblocks stay."

"It's been five hours since we turned over the money. If the kidnappers took off right away, they're long gone."

"They could be waiting until nightfall," Heflin said.

This was the first intelligent observation Heflin had made. "I agree."

"You do?"

"At night, surveillance from the chopper is worthless. It's easier to slip by unnoticed."

Heflin nodded. "What would you do?"

"My men know the territory. If you'll let me, I can coordinate the search for Joey and for the kidnappers. There's other manpower available. We can call in some of the volunteer search-and-rescue units."

Heflin shook his head back and forth, but he didn't say no.

Mace continued, "You met Barry, the night dispatcher."

"The bald guy?"

"He's a computer genius," Mace said. "He has the entire county on a grid. We'd work everything through him and—"

"Hold it! Are you telling me that your guy is better than my agents?"

"This isn't a damned game." Mace felt Heflin's resistance coming back. "Give me a chance. Let me try."

"Please," Nicole chimed in. "If there's any way to find Joey, we've got to do it."

"Joey's only chance is me," Heflin said. "What if

the kidnappers have already left this county? Then you'd have no jurisdiction.''

''Not a problem,'' Mace said. ''We have good relations with the state highway patrol, the surrounding counties and on the Ute reservation.''

''This is an FBI operation, Sheriff.'' Wearily Heflin stood. ''I'm in charge. I don't need your night dispatcher stepping in. A computer genius, my eye.''

A hopeless jackass. Heflin wasn't going to change his mind. ''All right, do it your way. But I'm going home, and I'm taking Nicole with me.''

He held her parka, and she quickly slipped into it. She was as anxious to leave as he was.

They were at the door when Heflin called out, ''Hey, Nicole.''

Wearily, she turned back toward him. ''Don't worry, Special Agent. I won't leave town.''

She stepped through the door with Mace. He was the one and only reason she was staying in Elkhorn. Because of him, running away was not an option. She'd worked hard to gain his trust and wouldn't betray him, wouldn't leave him. Their budding relationship promised a beautiful result, and she would not discard it lightly.

As she strode away from the Wentworth cabin, she hoped she would never have to return. She wanted to stay with Mace. At his ranch. She wanted to stay there forever.

When they were safely inside the Explorer with the doors closed and locked, he turned to her. ''Hell of a day.''

''You said it.''

''I talked to Jewel on the phone. She made a meat loaf for dinner.''

"Sounds heavenly," she said. Being alone with him felt ever so good. Despite her exhaustion and her worry, she smiled back at him. "I'll settle for a few hours without Heflin in my face, asking me the same questions over and over. He thinks I'm a criminal mastermind. Hah!"

Mace started up the car and threw it in reverse. "All things considered, you handled the situation well."

She sensed a hint of criticism. "Do you mean with Heflin's interrogation?"

"And during the ransom delivery," he said.

"There wasn't anything else I could do. I had to follow the kidnapper's instructions."

"I was there," he said as he pulled onto the main road. "I know what you went through."

Still, she heard hesitation in his voice. He didn't sound as if he wanted to give her a medal. "Do you think someone else could have done better?"

"I didn't say that."

"But you were thinking it. There weren't supposed to be any more secrets between us."

"Okay, here's my theory. You were set up. The kidnappers picked you to deliver the ransom because they were counting on your fear. They knew you'd believe their threats." He paused. "Did Joey know you'd been abused?"

Not this again! He simply wouldn't give up on his theory that Joey had participated in his own kidnapping. "Joey is a victim."

"Then where is he?"

She leaned back in the passenger seat, staring straight ahead. *Where was Joey?* When she talked to him on the phone, he sounded lighthearted and free.

She was sure he hadn't been faking. ''Why would he purposely stay in hiding?''

''Here's my theory,'' Mace said. ''Joey is choosing not to come forward because he got what he wanted.''

''The money?''

''You heard what Heflin said. Blake's business isn't doing well. If Joey asked for dough to pay off his gambling debts, Uncle Blake would've turned him down.''

For the first time, that reasoning made sense. She'd been fighting this logic since the moment Mace brought it up, but now she could see how Joey might have arranged his own abduction. Otherwise, he'd turn himself in.

During the past few days, he'd pleaded with her. Every time they'd talked, he begged her to follow the kidnapper's instructions. She'd thought he was scared, but it was just as likely that he wanted to make sure she gave them the ransom. He wanted the money—his share of the money. ''That little creep. That irresponsible, spoiled-brat, wannabe-artist, rich kid. I can't believe he'd do this to me.''

''He used your fear,'' Mace said.

Seriously angry, she clenched her fingers into fists. ''He used me.'' She pounded her fists on her thighs. ''He knew I'd be terrified of the threats, and he used my fear.'' She pounded once, twice, three times. ''Damn him!''

''I'm glad you're finally seeing reason.''

''He stole my savings,'' she growled. ''Two thousand bucks. Do you know how hard I had to work to save that nest egg? Do you have any idea how many hamburgers I had to serve?''

''Tons of burgers,'' Mace said.

"When I think of how he played me, I could kill him." She glanced over at Mace and noticed his huge grin. "What's so funny?"

"It's good to see you show your emotions," he said. "When you're really irate like this, what do you do?"

"I get myself under control."

"Do you ever get wild and drunk?" he asked.

"Never."

"Come on, Nicole. Do you scream? Break dishes?"

She never allowed her emotions to erupt. She felt as though, if she started screaming or breaking dishes, she wouldn't stop until she was hauled away in a straitjacket. "I'm not that sort of person."

"How do you let go?"

"There is one thing," she said sheepishly. "It's kind of like your battle cry."

"This battle cry?" He threw back his head. "Yi-yi-yi-yi."

"That's the one," she said.

"Well? What do you do to let off steam?"

She rolled her eyes. "I like to drive with all the windows open and the CD player blasting."

He turned on the road leading to the ranch house. "Let's do it."

"What do you mean?"

"Your car is gassed up and ready to roll. Let's go for a ride with the windows down."

Though it was dusk and chilly, that sounded like the most brilliant idea she'd ever heard. A sense of adventure cut through her outrage. "I should warn you that I sometimes sing along."

"The louder the better."

They parked in front of the ranch house. From inside, she saw the lights from the kitchen where Jewel was preparing meat loaf. The long, wood-frame house with a shake-shingle roof looked cozy and inviting. Perhaps they should just go inside and relax. That would be sensible and sane. "I feel ridiculous, Mace."

"Good," he said. "I want you to feel something. To feel everything."

"That's not how I am." But it sounded appealing. "At the very least I need a destination."

"Denver," he suggested.

"I can never go there," she said quickly. "That's where Derek is."

"How about Santa Fe?"

"Something closer," she said. "I know. We can go to the Elkhorn Café. They owe me a paycheck. Since that scumbag Joey stole all my money, I'm going to need every penny."

"You're on," he said. "We'll go for a wild and crazy drive to the Elkhorn Café."

When she slid into the driver's seat of her little Ford Escort, she felt good—even better when Mace planted himself in the passenger seat. Usually when she got behind the wheel, she was running away from something. Now she had a destination that was somehow more important than the café. And she had a partner, somebody who was riding shotgun, a buddy, a protector. She wasn't alone anymore.

Grinning, she adjusted the seat forward.

Mace fastened his seat belt. "The deputy who gassed up your car mentioned that the brakes seemed to be slipping."

"Not a chance," she said. "I keep my little car in excellent condition."

Too often, her survival had depended upon being able to make a quick escape. She turned the key in the ignition, and the engine hummed to life. It wasn't an expensive roar like Joey's BMW, but the familiar whirring filled her with satisfaction.

She glanced at the dashboard. Mace was right. The warning light for the brakes was on. It couldn't be anything serious. She'd had the car tuned up less than a month ago.

Mace had already put down his window. "Let's do it."

With her window down and her headlights on, she slipped in a tape. "It's ABBA," she said. "The old tunes are best for cruising."

When Mace started bobbing his head along to "Dancing Queen," he looked so adorable that she could hardly stand it. Who would've thought the sheriff had boogie in his soul?

She drove to the end of the driveway. The brakes did seem mushy, but they weren't going far—only to the Elkhorn Café and back. She made a left and gunned it.

The chilly evening breeze whipped through the car. Her troubles washed away. She turned up the volume and sang along. Laughter bubbled up inside her. She felt utterly, totally alive.

"I want to dance," she shouted.

"Anything you want," he yelled back. "Pull over. We'll do it right here."

When she pressed on the brakes, they were slow to catch, but then the car stopped. With the music still blaring, they jumped out.

She danced in the headlights. Her shoulders jiggled, and her hips swerved. Her arms waved over her head in time with the solid disco beat.

Mace tried a fancy turn that made her laugh. "Where'd you learn to do that?"

"Not at powwow," he said.

She danced closer to him. "You're pretty hip for a sheriff."

"You're just plain pretty."

She was in his arms. Her body pressed against his. She kissed him quickly, lightly, teasingly. Then she danced away. "Do you come here often?"

"Yeah, baby," he said. "What's your sign?"

"I'm not an easy pickup," she said. "I never kiss on the first date."

"I've got a lot more than kissing on my mind."

She was ready to make love with him, and she knew it would be different and better than anything she'd ever experienced before.

He caught hold of her hand, twirled her away from him, then pulled her close. Standing in the headlights, they kissed. His lips were warm in the cool Colorado night. Her heart beat even faster than the music. Fluttering like a butterfly broken free from its chrysalis, she soared high in the night, high as the stars.

When she looked up into his eyes, she felt a dreamy smile spread across her face.

"How do you feel?" he asked.

"Happy." Such a weird sensation after a day in hell. "I want to make love."

"Then it's unanimous."

"Let's go back to the house." She could hardly wait to get into his bed, to make love with him all night long.

They returned to her car. Before she whipped a U-turn, she checked in her rearview mirror. "That's strange. There's a car behind us. He's just sitting there with the lights off."

Mace swiveled around so he could see through the back window. "Damn."

"What is it?" Her excitement paled as she remembered the final threat from the kidnapper. He said he'd be watching and she could never be safe. "It's not them, is it?"

"I can't tell from this distance, but the shape is right. It might be the Jeep." He continued to peer into the gathering darkness. "I didn't notice that car when we drove this road before. Did you?"

"No," she said. Why was this happening now? What could they possibly want from her?

Mace pulled out his cell phone. In an instant he was talking to dispatch. His instructions were terse. "I think I've spotted the kidnappers. They're on the road leading to my house."

She turned off the tape. "Mace, what should I do?"

"Make a U-turn." His gun was in his hand.

"Really? You think I should drive toward them."

"I know you love this little car," he said. "But you can't outrun a three-legged heifer in this thing. Drive back to the house. We'll be safer inside."

Resentment cut through her—cold as the October wind. This wasn't fair! Every time she thought joy was within her grasp, she was disappointed.

Quickly she made her turn and drove directly at the waiting vehicle, directly toward danger. As she sped by them, her muscles tensed, and she waited for gunfire.

But nothing happened.

Mace turned around in his seat, keeping an eye on the Explorer. Quietly, he said. "They're turning. They're coming after us."

"That's crazy. Why would they take the risk of being so close to your house?" The logical answer flashed before her eyes. "Unless they don't plan to leave witnesses. They want to kill us."

"Keep going," he said. "It's less than a mile."

She could see the edge of his property. Her foot tapped the brakes. They were worse than loose. There was no response at all.

She jammed her foot to the floor. The car slowed slightly but not enough. "I can't make the turn."

"What?"

"My brakes don't work."

She swerved off the road. Bouncing over the shoulder and the rutted drainage ditch, she steered toward the lights of his ranch house. Her front fender crashed through the fence. The wood splintered across her hood, but she kept going, unable to stop. Her car bumped and jostled wildly across the uneven land until she plowed into a spruce tree beside the house. The air bags exploded.

Mace fought his way free. "Are you hurt?"

"I don't think so."

"Stay in the car." He was already out the door. Down on one knee, he aimed his handgun toward the road and fired three shots.

Slowly, he stood. "They're gone."

She unbuckled her seat belt and climbed out from behind the air bag. Her car was destroyed. Everything was ruined.

Chapter Thirteen

By the next morning, Nicole didn't feel a whole lot better. She stood in front of Mace's house with a mug of black coffee in one hand. With her other hand, she stroked the crumpled hood of her formerly perky blue sedan. The poor little thing was totaled.

This car had been good to her. She'd driven it across the country from San Francisco and used it to escape from Derek. Until last night, the Escort never let her down.

Now she was without transportation. Her low-cost, no-fault insurance wouldn't begin to pay for a replacement vehicle. And she had no savings, thanks to Joey.

Mace came up behind her. "It's hard to believe we got out of that wreck without injury."

"Apparently, crashing through the fence slowed us down." She sighed. "This is my fault. I should have known better than to drive with the 'check brakes' light on, but I had a tune-up recently and—"

"Before you start feeling too guilty, I should tell you that your brakes had been tampered with. One of the deputies who was here last night checked out your car. There were holes in the brake line, causing a slow drain. The more times you stepped on the brakes, the worse it got.''

''My car was sabotaged? How? It was parked in front of your house, and there were deputies all over the place.''

''Before we brought it here,'' Mace reminded her. ''It was sitting alone on the highway. Unprotected.''

She turned around to face him. If she had to get more bad news about her sabotaged car, she was glad that Mace was the messenger. Looking at him—even in these circumstances—gave her pleasure. The crisp October sunlight reflected off his shining black hair and rested gracefully on his broad shoulders. ''I bet you've got a theory about why somebody messed with my brakes.''

Though he wasn't smiling, he looked amused. ''You think I've got a theory, huh?''

''You always do.''

''Okay,'' he said. ''I figured out two possible reasons for sabotage—somebody didn't want you running off. Or they hoped to cause an accident.''

''Either way they got their wish.'' She should've been devastated, but when she was with Mace the world seemed like a more optimistic place. ''So, what else happened last night after I went to bed?''

''My deputies got here. We chased the bad guys.''

''Did you catch them?''

''Nope.'' After all his bragging to Heflin about how his men knew the territory, they'd lost the kidnappers. The beat-up Jeep Wagoneer had driven right up to his doorstep, and he let them get away. ''Three carloads of deputies. And we lost them.''

Mace figured they were still in this general area, parked in a barn or a garage. Or they might have gone into the foothills where they could dodge into a ravine or cover the car with tree branches.

As the FBI helicopter whirred overhead, he looked up. "We'll find them," he said.

"Whatever happened with that list of names and phone numbers from Joey's sketchbook?" she asked.

"Barry's still checking the phone numbers and not having much luck. Todd's number rings through to a woman who doesn't know anybody named Todd. George's phone is disconnected. Jimbo called from a pay phone at the airport."

"Frustration seems to be the theme for the day," she said. "Are you sure it was the kidnappers last night?"

He nodded. "I saw inside their car. They were wearing black ski masks."

When she shuddered, he lightly touched her shoulder. Last night, he thought. Last night, they'd been minutes away from making love. He regretted that missed opportunity more than anything else. There would always be another chance to nab the bad guys, but the moment had passed with Nicole. With this complicated woman, he was never sure when the right time would come again.

"How do you feel this morning?" he asked.

"Flustered. Frightened. And furious." The light in her blue eyes wavered. Somehow she managed to express all three of those emotions at once. "I don't understand why the kidnappers are coming after me."

"They want something from you," he said.

"But what? If they'd tell me, I'd be delighted to hand over whatever it is and get on with my life."

He suspected some kind of mind game. However, like Nicole, he couldn't figure out the whys and wherefores. "I think we'll have the answers when Joey turns up."

"I hate to admit it, but he must be behind this," she said. "I simply don't understand why he dislikes me so much."

"Don't waste your time trying to figure him out."

"Another theory?" she teased.

"I've been through police training and profiling so I know a little bit about psychology. It's my educated opinion that your former roommate, Joey, is nuttier than a pecan log."

"Very impressive analysis."

As they stood there face-to-face, it was easy for Mace to imagine that everything was right with the world. But he knew better. She was in the worst kind of danger, the kind that sneaks up without warning or apparent reason. "It's best if we make sure you're protected today. I want you to stay here at the ranch."

"Can't do it," she said. "My car is demolished. My savings are gone. I need to go to work."

"I admire your grit, but it's not necessary."

"It won't be a problem. Nothing bad is going to happen to me at the café, not with all those people around."

He lightly stroked her cheek. Her skin was soft as a rose petal. "Let me take care of you, Nicole."

"You've already done so much. You and Jewel." She closed her eyes and rubbed her face against his hand like a kitten wanting to be scratched behind the ears. "I don't want to be a freeloader."

He'd like to take care of her in so many ways, to treat her with the kindness she deserved. "Stay here today."

She captured his hand between both of hers. "It's

important for me to pay my own way. I learned that when I was with Derek. I need to go back to work. For my own self-respect.''

He couldn't argue with her. But he still didn't like it.

WHEN NICOLE STEPPED through the rear door leading into the kitchen of the Elkhorn Café, she was struck by the aroma of three-alarm chili on the stove and burgers on the grill.

Mace followed her inside. ''So this is where the magic happens.''

She inhaled deeply. ''Smell that?''

''Charbroil?''

''That's the scent of normalcy.''

Ever since she was sixteen, she'd worked in restaurants, ranging from diners to bistros to chic five-star eateries. She liked waitressing. The kitchens were warm and clean. Most patrons were hungry and, therefore, happy to see her when she came to their table. After she served their food, they forgot about her. That minimal amount of social interaction was perfect.

She took off her parka and hung it on a peg. This afternoon, after she helped Jewel in the barn, she'd cleaned one of her pink uniforms, including slacks and an apron. Again, normal. She was looking forward to spending the dinner hours here—performing her tasks competently and quietly without being the center of attention.

''Hey, Mike,'' she called to the cook.

He dropped his spatula, came out from behind the grill and gave her a big hug. ''I'm glad you're okay.''

This display of affection was so unusual that she could only stare at him, slack-jawed.

"Hey," Mace said. "Don't I get a big hug, too?"

"Not from me, wise guy."

"Then I'm going out front," Mace said. He pushed through one swinging door just as Deborah, the owner of the Elkhorn Café, charged through the other. As soon as she spied Nicole, she greeted her with gushy enthusiasm and a kiss on the cheek.

Suspiciously Nicole asked, "Why is everybody being so nice to me?"

"Because we care," Deborah said.

"No, really."

"We're dying to hear your side of the story," Deborah said. "Did you really deliver the ransom? Did you see the kidnappers?"

"That's right."

"And the Feds are giving you a hard time, those creeps." Her tanned, leathery face pulled into a scowl. Deborah was a hardworking woman who didn't put up with any nonsense. "Everybody around here is peeved about the Feds and all their nosy questions. As if we're giving those criminals a hideout?"

"Certainly not," Nicole said.

"We're on your side. We're with you and Mace." She picked up two plates. "Hey, I hear you two are getting hitched."

"No," she said. "We're friends."

"If I was you, sweetie, I'd grab him quick. He's a real catch." She winked. "We've got a big crowd tonight. Everybody's mad about this investigation stuff, and they want to talk about it."

Nicole grabbed her order pad and went through the door. The Elkhorn Café was full of people, and all of them were smiling at her. She could hardly walk from one booth to the next without being hugged and reassured.

She sidled up to Mace, who was sitting at the counter. She whispered, "I don't get it. All of a sudden, everybody's my friend."

"Did you win the lottery?" he whispered back.

"No."

"Then, it must mean that these people like you."

Two of his deputies—Philips and Greenleaf—regaled the crowd with a blow-by-blow account of how Nicole drove her car through Mace's fence and crashed into the cottonwood tree.

When she came to the table where Barry the dispatcher was sitting, he gently patted her hand. "You've done very well," he said.

"Thanks, I guess."

"She's the only good thing about this investigation," said Libby Tynsdale, owner of the infamous Elkhorn Lodge. "All those Feds? They're staying at my place, and I've never seen such a bunch of whiners. Can't lift a finger to take care of themselves."

There were murmurs of agreement.

"And it's not just them," Libby said. "That Blake Wentworth is a real piece of work. Always on his cell phone, yelling."

Barry the dispatcher asked, "Who's he talking to?"

"Must be an employee," Libby said. "He keeps yelling about how something got all goofed up. Only he doesn't say 'goofed.' I'm too much of a lady to repeat his profanity."

Barry exchanged a look with Mace. "Might be interesting to check out those phone records."

Glancing at this unprepossessing bald man, Nicole understood why Barry and Mace were good friends. Neither of them ever stopped being policemen, not even when they were eating dinner in a crowded restaurant. "What'll you have, Barry?"

"The usual." He smiled up at her. "You know, you and Mace look good together."

She tried to explain, "We're really not—"

"This is what I've heard," Libby cut in. "Daisy from Las Ranas says she's catering your wedding."

Deborah stepped up beside Nicole and snugged her arm around her waist. "I guess I'm going to be looking for another waitress soon."

"Actually," she said, "I need this job more than ever. I have to get a new car."

"Oh, my." Libby turned to Mace. "I don't think the sheriff would let his wife work."

"That's not his decision," Nicole returned.

Several people hooted as though they were privy to a private disagreement between her and Mace—an argument that didn't even exist.

Mace stood and goodnaturedly raised both hands. "That's enough, folks. I've got to take off. Don't give my girlfriend a hard time."

"Or you'll arrest us?" Libby questioned.

"I don't think there's a jail that could hold you, ma'am." As Mace went toward the door, he motioned to Philips and Greenleaf. "You two, come with me."

As long-haired Philips picked up his jacket, he said, "I told you she was spunky. Mace isn't going to be able to order her around."

"Speaking of orders," Nicole said as she stepped up to another table. "I'd better get busy or you're all going to starve."

When Nicole returned to the kitchen, she leaned against the stainless steel door to the walk-in refrigeration unit and took a couple of deep breaths. She'd never been a popular person, never been the belle of the ball. "I don't get it," she said aloud.

"Get what?" Deborah asked.

"Everybody being so…concerned."

"You're one of us, and you're in trouble. You need some kindness, sweetie."

"But nobody ever noticed me before."

"Well, it's like that with families. Nobody pays attention until there's a problem."

Families? Nicole knew nothing about families. She didn't have a real family after her father died. "But you people hardly know me."

"Mace knows you and likes you. That's enough for us. We're here to support you."

Though Nicole had known many people and had many connections, she'd never felt such a sense of belonging. The folks of Elkhorn were here for her, supporting her without question, despite her past. *It takes a village…* "Thanks, Deb."

"Now get back to work, sweetie." The café owner grinned. "We've got burgers to fry."

The rest of the evening passed in a cheerful blur. Nicole's natural reservoir of poise ran dry after a dozen more hugs and a lot of joking about the Feds. She joined in the laughter with the openness of a child. Her barriers were gone. She felt unconditionally accepted, warmed to the soul.

At about nine o'clock, she made the trek out back to carry a bag of garbage to the dumpster at the edge of the parking lot. A residual smile played across her lips as she lifted her face and allowed the cold night air to refresh her. After she tossed the garbage, closing and locking the dumpster lid so the raccoons and tree squirrels wouldn't get into the food scraps, she stared up into velvet black skies sprinkled with stars. So peaceful.

Before moving here, she expected to be bored in a small town. But the quiet soothed and refreshed her. The always-changing view of the mountains provided plenty of entertainment.

When Nicole heard someone approaching, she turned with a grin, ready to chat.

She faced the tall man in the black ski mask.

"We meet again," he said.

Before she could scream, he grabbed her and jammed a white cloth over her mouth. A foreign, antiseptic smell stung her nostrils. A drug? Chloroform?

She struggled, trying not to inhale. But she could already feel her strength fading. She was dizzy, losing consciousness.

WHEN SHE AWOKE, her eyelids felt gummy. Her mouth tasted like cotton. Nicole was aware of being outside, lying in the dirt. An Army blanket had been tossed over her, but she was freezing cold.

When she sat up, her head throbbed. Where was she? What had happened?

It hardly mattered. She pulled the blanket over her head and huddled miserably on the cold, damp earth.

She'd been snatched by the kidnappers, and they brought her here. Were they still here, waiting for her to awaken? Cautiously she listened. Though the inside of her skull hammered, she could hear no other sounds except the whisper of wind and the undefinable skittering of nocturnal creatures.

She peeked out from the blanket. Boot Hill!

The aged grave markers and crumbling tombstones surrounded her like a silent army of death. She'd been brought here to die. Or maybe she was dead already. When she stood, the mysterious ghostwalkers would lead her on an endless, lonely path. She would become the horrifying creature in Joey's painting.

Don't be a fool! You're not dead! Dead people don't breathe, they don't feel the cold.

Gathering her courage, she rose. Her legs were still weak, and she almost fell. Bracing her arms against a tombstone, Nicole waited until her breathing was more regular. She took one step, then another.

Silently she offered apologies to the spirits whose graves she trod upon, but she didn't have the strength to show proper respect. She needed to leave this place. Mace must be worried about her.

The thought of him gave her encouragement. Somehow he would find a way to protect her. Oh, gosh, he was going to be angry that she'd gotten herself captured. This morning he'd warned her.

But how could she have anticipated this?

She remembered her dream, the body hanging from the tree limb. Slowly she lifted her gaze. She turned toward the cottonwoods at the edge of Boot Hill. If she saw someone hanging there, she would run. She wouldn't confront the vision of her own mortality.

The trees stretched bony fingers toward the starry skies, but there were no skeletons. The cottonwoods were only trees with branches and roots. She was here. In a real, tangible world. Here. And alive.

But she needed to be somewhere else, somewhere warm, somewhere with people. There was nothing nearby. Boot Hill lay halfway between Las Ranas and Elkhorn.

The only sensible action was to start walking, stepping around the gravestones, heading toward the gate in the fence that encircled the cemetery.

She glanced toward the corner of Boot Hill where Mace had found evidence, a tube of acrylic paint. He looked so handsome that day—the day she kissed him for the first time. She held his image in her mind, warding off all the bad things that had happened to her. If she could think only of Mace, she might find the strength to go forward.

Her hand touched the top of the gate and froze. Outside the fence, leaning against the weathered wooden pickets, she saw a man sitting with his legs stretched out in front of him. His head drooped as if he'd nodded off. Had he been left behind to guard her?

She ducked down behind the gate. Peering through the dark, she recognized the narrow shoulders and thin neck. It was Joey.

Did she dare to approach him? If Mace's theories were correct, Joey was on the side of the kidnappers. He might have ordered them to bring her here for a final meeting with him.

He wasn't moving, must be sleeping soundly. And that would be typical of Joey, dragging her here in the cold and then falling asleep.

She pushed through the gate and stalked toward him. "Joey."

He didn't move a muscle, even though she was directly in front of him. "Joey."

Something was wrong.

She knelt beside him. The blanket fell from her shoulders as she reached for him.

His head lolled back. His jacket fell open, and she saw the blood. He'd been wounded. His chest was covered with blood.

Was he still alive? She felt for a pulse. His flesh was ice-cold. His long slender fingers were stiff.

Joey was dead.

Chapter Fourteen

The parking lot behind the Elkhorn Café was a crime scene. As such, it should be treated carefully, following routine procedures. Mace knew the drill. He'd taught his deputies how to use the proper investigative techniques and tools: question the witnesses; observe the scene; take photographs; collect forensic evidence. Most important was attitude. The lawman on the scene needed to maintain control of the situation, to stay calm in the face of danger.

But Mace found it nearly impossible to take his own advice. Leaving Barry in charge, he stood brooding in dark silence. His back leaned against his vehicle. His arms were folded across his chest so nobody would notice that his hands were shaking from a combination of unexpressed anger and guilt. He couldn't think, couldn't reason. Nicole was gone.

Nearly an hour ago, according to witness reports, she stepped outside the café to dump the garbage and she never returned. When he first saw her little red parka, hanging limp from a peg by the back door of the café, a blinding rage exploded behind his eyes. The shock and pain were physical—like being struck between the eyes by a bolt of lightning.

It took all his strength and self-control not to lash out at his deputies—Philips and Greenleaf—who were supposed to be keeping an eye on her. Instead of watching the doors, they'd gone back inside for a coffee and a slice of pecan pie.

But his anger at them was nothing compared to his own self-disgust. He should have known better than to let her out of his sight. All his promises to protect her were nothing more than empty, futile words. He'd failed. And Nicole was paying the price.

All the activity in the parking lot, the flashing lights from deputy's cars and aggressive shouting of questions ought to produce some clues leading to a search, but Mace wasn't hopeful. The kidnappers had eluded them at every turn. They knew how to use the vast, open landscape, disappearing like rattlesnakes slithering into their lairs. They'd taken Nicole from him. If they hurt her…

What could he do? He was stuck here without a clue, helpless and bereft.

Barry approached him. His round body moved with a sense of purpose. His beard bristled. "We got a lead."

"What is it?"

"Somebody reported an explosion," he said. "There's a car on fire in a gully near Las Ranas. The guys on the scene say it's a Jeep Wagoneer like the one the kidnappers have been driving."

Though Mace dreaded the answer, he had to ask the question. "Any victims?"

"None."

"Let's go." Mace yanked open the driver's side door to his vehicle. There was no point in staying here; Nicole wasn't in this area.

Barry climbed into the passenger seat and used the police radio to inform dispatch that they were headed toward Las Ranas.

Mace hit the road outside Elkhorn at top speed with his flashers going. Though this might be nothing but another dead end, it felt good to be in motion.

"You investigated in Las Ranas before," Barry said. "Who'd you talk to?"

"Don Blackbird." That was the afternoon when Nicole first kissed him. He licked his lips, remembering the honeyed taste of her mouth.

"Right," Barry said. "You filed a report. You found out that Joey owes money at the casinos."

Mace didn't give a damn about Joey, except as he related to Nicole.

Barry continued, "Those debts are a good motive for Joey staging his own abduction. I'm also thinking Blake Wentworth might be involved. I'll check out the calls he made on his cell phone. You think?"

"Don't care." Mace careered down the relatively straight stretch of road. "I don't give a damn about the kidnapping."

"Because you're worried about Nicole," Barry said.

"Damn right."

"Then you need to start thinking like a cop. That's what she needs right now. A good, smart cop who can figure out where she is and who took her."

He was right. Mace needed to stop feeling and start thinking. His intuition and logic were the best way to find her, but his brain was still in shock. "Okay, partner. Help me out. What should I do?"

"You could start by slowing down."

Mace glanced down at the dashboard. The speedometer needle was buried on the high end.

"I know we're in a hurry," Barry said, "but if you crash into an elk on the road, you'll total this vehicle, and I don't want to process the paperwork."

Mace eased up on the gas pedal. "Better?"

"You bet."

But his brain still wasn't working. "Talk to me."

"Let's think about Las Ranas. Why would the kidnappers be there? There was something else in your report about a tube of paint or something."

"I found it at Boot Hill," Mace said. "Joey used to go there to paint. He used it for the background in that sick portrait of Nicole."

In his mind he could see her walking amid the tombstones and tidying the gravesites. Later, she'd dreamed about Boot Hill. "For some reason, that site was important to Joey."

He slammed on the brakes and whipped into a U-turn. "We'll go there first."

NICOLE TRIED to arrange Joey's body, and covered him with the blanket that had been left for her by the kidnappers. His death should be respected. It seemed cruel to leave him here alone, propped against the weathered fence enclosing Boot Hill.

She whispered a prayer for him. His life had been troubled. Perhaps in death he would find peace. She hoped Joey would become a guardian angel instead of a ghostwalker, an uneasy spirit seeking revenge.

Quietly she offered her own eulogy. "You were a good friend to me, Joey. I'll never forget you."

She stood and took a step backward. Though still a little dizzy, the hammering inside her skull had faded to a dull ache. Her arms wrapped tightly around her midsection. In her lightweight pink uniform, she had scant protection against the night chill. Maybe she'd freeze to death. Somewhere she'd heard that hypothermia was a peaceful way to die.

Her gaze lifted toward the old tombstones. When she'd come here with Mace, she'd seen a stark charm in this setting. She understood why Boot Hill might fascinate an artist like Joey.

After the nightmare, her perception changed. Buried here, beneath ancient markers, were many of her fears, reminders of pain and her own mortality. But she didn't want her life to end. Not now, when she finally had something to live for.

The snap of a twig startled her. "Who's there?"

She was answered by an eerie rush of wind. The bare branches of the cottonwoods created moving shadows, stirring her darkest memories of terror and abuse. She remembered the quiet footstep in the hallway before the door crashed open. Derek's soft voice as his caresses became hurtful.

Stepping backward again, she stumbled, catching herself before she tumbled down the embankment. Was there a threat? Were the kidnappers nearby? She almost wished they'd attack. Anything would be better than waiting for the next blow to fall.

More noise came from the dry creekbed. The dried grasses crackled.

They were coming for her.

She had to run. Her only defense was escape. She'd been here before. She knew she couldn't face them and win.

Her feet felt heavy as hardened cement. Her strides seemed slow motion and awkward as she dodged down the hill toward the road. But that was the worst possible route. If she stayed on the road, she'd be easy to find. That must have been what happened to Joey. After he called her and said he was okay, the kidnappers must have returned and picked him up. Then they killed him.

His murder was her fault. She should have known better than to turn over the ransom before Joey was delivered safely. But there was no time now for guilt. She had to keep going or be killed herself. And she needed to get off the road.

Looking down, she saw the white of her apron. In the night, it gleamed like a beacon. She tore off the scrap of material and threw it to the ground.

She fought for every step, dragged her feet, staggering blindly, putting distance between herself and Boot Hill.

MACE WAS THANKFUL for Barry and his sane advice. The best way to help Nicole was to be a good cop. That's what Mace had to do. Purposefully he shut down the emotional storm that drenched his brain. The light of clarity grew within him. He became a hunter.

Trusting his gut instinct, he drove toward Boot Hill. This wasn't the most logical place to find Nicole, but none of the kidnappers' behavior made sense. Why had they taken her?

He posed the question to Barry, who thoughtfully stroked his beard. "Doesn't make a trickle of sense to me. It's not like this was a political kidnapping where they were trying to make a statement. They wanted a ransom and they got their money."

"That's when it should have been over," Mace

said. "Messing around with Nicole means taking an extra risk. Why would they do it?"

Grabbing Nicole had caused the entire county to mobilize. Everybody was looking for her. Which meant, Mace realized, that they weren't looking for the kidnappers. "A distraction," he said. "They grabbed Nicole so all our forces would be diverted. We'd all be busy looking for her."

"You shut down the roadblocks?"

Mace nodded. The instant he heard Nicole was missing, he pulled in every lawman and volunteer who could help with search.

"That's probably why they set fire to their own vehicle," Barry said. "Another distraction."

"Call Heflin," Mace said. "Tell him to double up on his search. If the kidnappers waited until now to make their move, they can't be more than an hour away from Elkhorn."

He turned off his flashers about a mile before they reached Boot Hill. He parked beside the dry creekbed and left the vehicle. In the darkness his senses sharpened. He heard the small sounds of night—the wind beneath a raptor's wing, the scurrying of night animals. The air smelled moist and putrid, like the stink of ancient, rotting corpses. Peering toward the cemetery, he saw a shape more solid than the bare branches of shrubs.

"Over there." He pointed, then ran toward the motionless form. His boots dug into the hard earth, churning up bits of loose rock.

Leaning against the fence was a body. *Not Nicole. Please don't let this be Nicole.*

Mace tore off an Army blanket covering the body of Joey Wentworth. His hands were in his lap, but the placement was strange. It looked like someone had tried to pose him after rigor mortis set in. His stringy hair had been brushed off his forehead.

Barry huffed and puffed as he came up the hill. "I'm not used to this physical stuff. I want to get back behind my desk."

"Meet Joey." Mace hadn't really known Joey Wentworth when he was alive. From what Nicole had told him, they wouldn't have liked each other, but Mace regretted this young man's passing. Any senseless death counted as a tragedy.

"We need to let the Feds know," Mace said. "But I don't want them distracted from their search for the kidnappers. Give them half an hour to get in position, then call."

"Are you sure?" Barry asked.

"That's my decision," Mace said. "This is a murder in Sterling County. It's my jurisdiction."

He entered the cemetery carefully, looking for Nicole. There were no signs of life here.

Though the earth was too hard to take footprints, he went down on one knee and studied the ground, looking for a pattern. Years of hunting on the rez with Tata Charlie taught him how to follow the spoor, how to read the patterns. There were broken stems of dried grass. He followed the trail to a larger depression. Reaching down, he touched the spot. A body might have rested here, possibly Joey. Some person or persons had walked in and out. One of them might have been Nicole.

The way Joey's body had been arranged and the thoughtfulness of placing a blanket over a dead man reminded him of her reverence for the dead. His instinct told him that she'd been here. And now she was on the run.

There was only one road leading past this spot. She had to take it.

He charged down the hill.

"Where are you going?" Barry called out.

"I think Nicole was here. She might have tried to tidy up the body. Which indicates that—at that time—she was alone."

"Where is she now?"

Mace reached the road. He saw a flash of white on the shoulder and ran toward it. Nicole's apron!

She was headed south. If she was running, she'd cover a lot of ground. He needed to drive.

When he opened the car door, Barry yelled, "Hey, you're not leaving me here, are you?"

"Somebody has to stay with the body."

"I don't even have my gun with me. What am I going to do if the kidnappers show up?"

"Talk them to death." Mace unholstered his gun and tossed it toward Barry. "Now you're armed."

As he drove slowly, he turned on the police siren and the flashers as a signal for Nicole. If she was hiding, the noise and lights ought to draw her out.

He crept along the road. One mile. Then two. There were no houses. No signs of civilization except for a barb wire fence at one side of the road.

Leaving the flashers on, he parked the vehicle, got out and walked along the road, staring into the trees on the unfenced side. "Nicole! Are you out here?"

He went farther. With every step, he felt closer to her. If he'd believed in such things, he might have thought they were communicating telepathically. Finally he heard a weak shout.

"Nicole?"

There was a rustling in the underbrush. He turned and saw her. Her pink uniform was smeared with dirt. Her arms were scratched from tree branches, and she was nearly blue from the cold.

He'd never seen a more beautiful sight.

Before she dropped, he rushed to her and lifted her into his arms. Her body was freezing cold. First thing was to get her warmed up. He carried her toward his vehicle. In his search for her, he'd come a longer distance than he'd realized, but holding her small, fragile body was no strain. He tried to hurry, being careful not to jostle her too much.

"I thought…" She gasped. Her eyelids closed. "I thought they were coming after me."

"Are you injured?" he asked. "Did they hurt you?"

"Drugged," she said. "Something smelly over my nose. Didn't want to inhale."

Heartless bastards! They drugged her and dumped her at the cemetery, left her to freeze. All for the sake of a distraction. "You're going to be all right."

"I found Joey," she murmured. "It's all my fault. He's dead."

"Don't blame yourself. You didn't do anything wrong."

"If I'd been smarter about the ransom—"

"No." He wouldn't allow her to take even one baby step down this path. "You have no reason to feel guilty."

They reached the car, and he placed her in the back seat, tore off his shearling coat and wrapped it around her. He stroked her cheek, and she shivered violently. Her skin was clammy.

"I should take you to the hospital," he said.

She smiled weakly. "You said that to me the first time we met. Take me to the hospital."

"It might be best."

"I'll be okay." She shook her head. "Jewel can help me. I want to go home."

For the first time in hours Mace relaxed. She'd said "home." She thought of his ranch as home.

When he gathered her against him, it was for his own reassurance. Her arms were limp, but she would recover, she'd regain her strength and be all right. "I'll never let you out of my sight again."

A deputy's car pulled up beside them, and Barry got out. When he saw Nicole, a benevolent grin spread across his round, bearded face. "How's she doing?"

"Half-frozen," Mace said. "I'm taking her home with me."

"You stay in the back," Barry said. "I'll drive."

Within minutes they were on their way. Mace cradled Nicole against him. Her eyes were closed. She was resting.

Barry said, "I'll put in a call to the doc and have him meet us at your place."

"Good idea." Mace spoke softly so he wouldn't disturb Nicole. "How did you get backup?"

"I had my cell phone," Barry said. "You really didn't think I'd sit out in the cold waiting for you?"

"Guess not."

"And I put in the call to Heflin about finding Joey. You're going to have a battle with the Feds."

A fight over jurisdiction was to be expected, but Mace didn't expect much of a struggle. Heflin had failed on all three criteria for a kidnap operation: the victim was dead; the ransom was gone; the perpetrators were likely to escape.

It didn't get much worse than that. Since the FBI had been in charge, they'd lost all credibility.

"Heflin was right about one thing," Mace said. "He kept insisting that the kidnappers were professional criminals."

"But you didn't think so," Barry said.

"I kept noticing the amateurish stuff. The torn-up cabin. The weird midnight meeting with Nicole." He thought for a moment. "Even screwing around with the brake line on her car seemed childish."

But their subsequent behavior had been ruthless. Joey was murdered in cold blood. They'd torched their own vehicle. These were the acts of pros—men who operated without conscience.

"With any luck," Barry said, "they've got a criminal record. If we find forensic evidence in the burned-out Jeep, we'll want to use the FBI crime lab."

"I've got no problem with cooperating," Mace said. "That's all I wanted from the start."

But he didn't intend to worry about the investigation now. His entire focus was on the woman who leaned against him. He wanted to make her world a safe, secure place. He wanted to end all her nightmares and give her sweet dreams.

She was so precious. She'd gone through so much. And, he realized, she would never feel truly safe until Joey's murderers were apprehended.

Chapter Fifteen

After two days in bed, Nicole was more than recovered from her superficial bumps and bruises, but Mace insisted on treating her like an invalid. He wouldn't even let her walk out to the barn unless he stuck to her side like flypaper—a particularly handsome scrap of flypaper, but annoying nonetheless.

It wasn't that she didn't enjoy being with him, but she was anxious to return to a real-life routine, helping Jewel with chores, going back to work at the café and saving up for a car. She wanted something real with Mace, too.

Propping herself up against the pillows, she decided that this was the morning she'd assert her independence. Though the outside world was a dangerous place where the kidnappers were still at large, she couldn't stay locked up forever like Rapunzel with her long golden hair. All the attention had been pleasant, and she deeply appreciated the ''get well'' flower bouquets from Deputies Philips and Greenleaf, from the gang at the Elkhorn Café, from Daisy at Las Ranas and from Barry. But it was time to move on.

There was a tap on her bedroom door, and she called out, ''Come in.''

Mace entered, carrying two coffee mugs. One for him. One for her. He placed her mug on the bedside table. "How do you feel this morning?"

"Fine."

He leaned down and lightly kissed her forehead. All this gentleness had to change. Her enforced closeness to Mace without *really* touching him was driving her mad. She wanted *real* kisses—deep, hard kisses that she could feel all the way to her toes. She wanted to make love to him. But that was impossible while they were surrounded by dozens of caretakers. If they made love now, she'd feel like the entire population of Elkhorn was watching.

She picked up her morning coffee and took a sip. "How's the investigation going? Any developments overnight?"

He nodded. His dark eyes glistened warmly, but she sensed an underlying nervousness. Over the past few days, she'd become expert in reading every nuance of his mood. She asked, "Bad news?"

"The opposite. Remember how I told you that we found a set of fingerprints on the burned-out vehicle?"

"On the gas cap. It was very clever of your men to look there."

"We have an ID," he said. "It's a guy with a criminal record as long as my arm. The police in Denver have taken him into custody."

This was wonderful news, but Mace didn't sound too happy. "What's the problem?"

"He has an airtight alibi for part of the time he was supposed to be here in Elkhorn. The cops are still holding him, but one fingerprint isn't enough to make a case against him for kidnapping."

"How's Heflin taking this?"

"He's back in Denver, too."

She could tell something was bothering him. "Does it upset you that the momentum of the investigation has shifted to Denver?"

"Not really," he said. "Like most folks around here, I'll be glad when we're left alone to handle our own business."

"I feel that way, too." Now was a perfect opening to tell him that she had to get out of bed. "It's time for me to stand on my own two feet. I need to get out of the house."

"That's what I wanted to hear."

"It is?" She was perplexed.

"Because I want to take you to Denver."

The air squeezed out of her lungs. "I can't go there. Derek is in Denver."

"I know how you feel," Mace said, "but it's important to the case against this kidnapper that you go to Denver. You're the only witness, Nicole."

"I didn't see anybody's face," she protested. She didn't want to go to Denver. She couldn't possibly be safe in that town. Derek would find her and tear her transient happiness to shreds.

"The Denver PD wants you to do a voice lineup."

"What's that?"

"It's like a visual lineup. You sit behind a protective screen. Nobody can see you. And you listen to several voices saying the same thing. If you can pick the kidnapper out of the lineup, it's another piece of evidence they can use against him."

"I still don't like the idea." But how could she refuse? She wanted the kidnappers behind bars. "But I guess I don't have a choice."

Mace stood. "We leave in half an hour."

"Wait a minute. Why were you so sure I'd go along with this plan?"

He paused at the door to her bedroom. "The sooner we put the bad guys in jail, the sooner you'll feel safe."

As if she'd ever feel safe. The threat would always be alive in her memory. Fear was her constant companion. It had always been so.

Though the kidnappers had terrorized her, drugged her and left her to freeze in a cemetery, she was one hundred times more frightened of Derek. And now she was returning to his realm.

AFTER HITCHING A BOUNCY ride in a twin-engine airplane, she and Mace disembarked at Centennial Airport at the south end of town. She was back in Denver, the scene of her disastrous marriage. But this time she wasn't alone.

Mace was never more than three feet from her. Though he was armed and carried his badge in his wallet, he didn't look like the sheriff of the Western version of Mayberry, RFD. He wore his city clothes— a black business suit and polished loafers instead of cowboy boots. Still, no woman in her right mind would mistake him for an urban businessman. Mace radiated virility. The collar of his blue shirt was open, and she could see the gleam of his silver bear necklace, a symbol of protection. When he walked, he moved with the confident stride of a conquering hero. His dark eyes were in constant motion, scanning for threats. All in all, he looked untamed, like a sleek alpha male wolf in sheep's clothing.

She had also changed from her standard blue jeans

and sweater for the Denver trip. She wore her one and only skirt—a plaid wool A-line, midcalf—and a blue sweater. She'd fastened her hair on top of her head in a fashionably messy bun. She'd even put on lipstick and a bit of mascara.

"You look pretty," Mace said.

"You clean up pretty well yourself, Sheriff. Where'd you get the outfit?"

"I used to dress like this all the time when I worked for Denver PD."

"Even with the necklace?"

He nodded. "Turquoise and the bear are good luck, and a cop needs all the luck he can get."

As they drove toward downtown in a rental car, Mace sprang another surprise. "We'll stay here tonight."

"In Denver? Why?"

"For one thing, it's already two o'clock in the afternoon. We won't get done with the lineup until five o'clock. Then it's too late to fly back to Elkhorn."

"What's the other thing?" she asked suspiciously.

"While we're here, I want to talk to Blake Wentworth again. I have a few questions for him."

She grumbled, "This is a new theory, isn't it? You think Blake was involved with the kidnappers."

"He makes a good suspect," Mace said. "His oil exploration business has suffered recent setbacks, and all that money was sitting there in Joey's trust fund. I can see how Blake might have arranged this to get his hands on a share of the cash."

"Surely you don't believe he killed Joey." Though she certainly wasn't fond of Blake, who had been nothing but rude to her, she didn't think he was the sort of vicious monster who would callously arrange for his own nephew's brutal murder. "I think Blake liked Joey. He encouraged him in his artwork."

"We traced those phone calls he made to Denver," Mace said. "Three times he called an untraceable phone with a Denver prefix and talked for a total of thirty-three minutes."

"How could a phone be untraceable?"

"It's like the cell phones the kidnappers used, registered to a person who doesn't exist," Mace said. "He's explained all this to the Denver cops, but I want to ask the questions myself."

She settled back in the passenger seat and watched through the windshield as the suburban streets near Centennial Airport became progressively more urban in character. Her home with Derek had been in the upscale central area near the Denver Country Club where some of the stately mansions had been in the same family for more than a hundred years. Old money.

She knew that Blake Wentworth lived farther southwest in a relatively affluent suburb. Joey had told her that his uncle had picked a modest house close to his divorced wife and their three children. Would a cold-blooded murderer stay in contact with his family?

"There's a third thing," Mace said. "One more reason I want to stay in Denver overnight."

"What's that?"

"Alone time. Just you and me. I want one night when we can be together without my sister, ten deputies and half the population of Elkhorn looking over our shoulders."

Her heart lifted. "I like thing number three."

He glanced over at her and smiled. "I hoped you would."

When she smiled back, he didn't see a bit of wariness. He loved to see her smile. Nicole had changed so much since he first picked her up off the floor in the Wentworth cabin. Her fears weren't gone, but they were quiet. Her confidence was real instead of a prissy princess act to keep outsiders away.

He was so eager about being with her tonight that he hardly gave a damn about the lineup and pursuing his investigation with Blake. Tonight belonged to him and Nicole.

In downtown Denver, he pulled into a familiar space outside the police headquarters. This wasn't the first time he'd been back since he was elected sheriff of Sterling County. He'd stayed on decent terms with the guys in the big city, and they all pretty much agreed that Mace was a lot easier to handle as an ex-detective than when he and Barry built their reputation as two cops who never knew when to quit.

Inside the station, he introduced Nicole to a couple of guys he'd worked with. He said she was a friend.

"A good friend?" one of them asked.

"I hope so," she responded.

"Tell me this," the Denver detective said. "Does Mace still come up with a theory for every crime?"

She grinned. "You bet he does."

"Oh, man!" The detective rolled his eyes. "He used to make me nuts with all his crime theories. He sounded like Sherlock Holmes himself."

"Elementary," Mace said. And maybe this time he'd found the evil genius worthy of his deductive skills. It was hard to imagine a crime more compli-

cated than the abduction and murder of Joey Wentworth.

When Nicole was shown into the lineup room
where she'd hear several different voices and, with
luck, come up with a positive identification, he continued his shop talk, reviewing old cases. Successes
and screw-ups. But his heart wasn't in the good-
natured joking. Even though Nicole was completely
safe and in the company of other law officers, he
didn't like being away from her. Not even for a few
minutes.

Also, his entire being focused on what would happen later tonight. He'd already made the hotel reservations and arranged for a suite. That way, if things
didn't work out, he could sleep on the sofa. Mace
sure as hell hoped not. In the past few days he'd taken
more cold showers than a rainbow trout.

She came out of the lineup room and flashed a
brilliant smile. For a second he thought she might run
across the room and throw herself into his arms. But
Nicole was still too reserved for that kind of outward
display.

"She nailed him," the investigating officer said.
"Perfect identification. We'll hold him here until you
and the FBI figure out what to do with him."

Nicole stepped up close beside him and slipped her
hand into his. "I knew his ugly voice as soon as I
heard it. Finally I feel like I've done something useful."

"And that deserves a celebration." Mace nodded
to the other cops. "Sorry, boys. You aren't invited."

NICOLE DIDN'T TELL MACE that the hotel he'd chosen
for their alone time was the place where she'd suf-

fered one of her most horrible evenings with Derek. In the banquet room her husband had received an award for some kind of phony achievement, and she'd received a punishment when they returned to their home.

It had been less than a year ago, but the hotel seemed very different when she swept through the revolving door on the arm of her studly lawman. The lights in the lobby didn't glare so brightly. The air seemed warmer.

Since there was only one suitcase between them, they didn't wait for a bellboy. Mace escorted her to the elevators, and they rode to the twelfth floor.

Their suite was beautifully furnished in Danish modern with fresh flowers on the coffee table in front of the sofa.

Mace turned to her. "What should we do for dinner?"

She hung the Do Not Disturb sign on the doorknob before closing it and purred, "Room service."

"Are you sure? We're in the big city. I'm pretty sure we can get something gourmet and not fried."

"I'm not hungry. I'd rather be alone with you."

"You're not too tired?"

"Perfectly fine," she said.

"Good." He pulled her into his arms and kissed her with all the passion she'd been waiting for. The pressure of his mouth against hers was fierce but exquisitely tender. Their bodies fitted together like two halves made whole.

Trailing kisses to her ear, he nibbled on the lobe and whispered, "I'm pretty hungry."

"I'm starved."

He leaned back to look into her face. His head

cocked to one side. His dark eyes absorbed her, drawing her inexorably closer, making her a part of him. She reached up and touched his bronzed cheekbone, traced the firm line of his jaw. Her thumb played across his lips.

"We should call for food," he said. "I have a feeling I might need my strength tonight."

"Let me order." She went to the phone beside the sofa. Without consulting a menu, she ordered filet mignon, medium rare, with asparagus and pasta. A bottle of burgundy wine. And flan with caramel icing and dark chocolate for dessert.

"Sounds good," he said. "How'd you know what to ask for?"

"Lucky guess." She hung up the phone. "I haven't spent my whole adult life working in restaurants without learning a little bit about food."

He took off his suit jacket and sat on the sofa beside her. "Tell me what happened in the lineup at headquarters."

"Everyone was very polite and introduced themselves—a couple of cops and a couple of attorneys. They asked me what the guys in the lineup should say—something I'd heard them say before."

Two phrases had stuck in her mind. She'd played them on an endless loop, hoping that, with repetition, they would lose their ability to scare her. "When he saw me outside the café, he said, 'We meet again.'" As soon as she spoke the words, she heard the echo of the kidnapper's voice, a hateful sound.

"What else?" Mace asked.

The other threat came when she was delivering the ransom in the convenience store rest room. "He said, 'If you tell him, you're both going to die.' I'll never forget how terrified I was. I was sure he'd kill me. And you, too.''

''But he didn't,'' Mace said.

She hadn't wanted to relive those dark moments, but she couldn't erase her memories. ''He killed Joey, instead.''

Mace wrapped his arm around her shoulders and held her for several moments, allowing time for the fear to dissipate. Softly he said, ''You've been through a lot of trauma.''

She'd been shaken to the depths of her soul. Not even a lifetime of abuse could have prepared her for the terrifying regime of the kidnappers—from her ransacked cabin to the ransom delivery to that surreal night at Boot Hill. ''I'm glad I didn't have to do it by myself. If it weren't for you, I'd be a total wreck.''

''I don't believe it.'' He nuzzled behind her ear. ''You're stronger than you look.''

Though his little kisses felt good, she stopped him. She held his face between her hands. ''There's something I need to tell you, Mace. Tonight I expect to make love to you. I want you to know that I'm doing this for all the right reasons.''

''What reasons are those?''

''Because I care about you. I feel a deep…'' She hesitated, trying to find exactly the right word. Was it love? Somehow the time wasn't exactly right to say that word. There were a few barriers left between them. ''I feel a deep affection for you.''

''Okay, princess.'' He enfolded her hands in his. ''Same here. And no more lies.''

''Right.''

''Since we're making confessions, there's something I ought to tell you.'' His eyes were warm.

"Ever since I first met you, I've been fascinated by one thing. Nicole, will you take down your hair for me?"

"My pleasure."

She rose to her feet and circled the coffee table to stand in front of him. Maintaining direct and slightly sexy eye contact, she reached up and pulled out the pins that held her bun in place. One by one she removed the fasteners.

Intently he watched her every move. His lips parted. His breathing quickened. His barely suppressed arousal excited her, as well.

Finally her long blond hair was free. She shook her head and the long tresses cascaded past her shoulders to her waist in a shimmering, silky curtain.

"Turn around," he said in a husky voice.

She spun in a quick circle, and her hair swirled.

"Slower," he said.

She enjoyed enticing him. She craned her neck as she turned and peeked over her shoulder at him.

"Come here," Mace ordered.

As soon as she was close, he dragged her down onto his lap. He buried his fingers in her hair, smoothing the strands, pulling gently until her head tilted back.

His kiss was slow and sensuous, thoroughly exploring her mouth. His hands caressed her through her clothing, as though they were making out. Though it had been long ago since she'd lost her virginity, she felt as though this was truly the first time she'd made love.

When their room service arrived, Mace whipped the cart inside, tipped the waiter and rushed him out the door. He stood beside her at the sofa and held out his hand. "Come with me to the bedroom."

"But we should eat dinner while it's hot."

"I'm hungry for you."

How could she refuse? She took his hand, following him into the hotel bedroom.

His hands were fast and sure, as he unbuttoned his shirt and tore it off, exposing his smooth, sienna chest and muscular torso. When she tried to be equally quick, he caught her hands. "Let me."

He lifted her sweater slowly, gliding it up and over her head, untangling the material from her hair. He removed her skirt, her slip, her bra. Then, finally, his trousers. They stood naked before each other, except for the silver necklace he always wore. The cool metal gleamed. The bear totem rested in the hollow of his throat.

She placed her hand on his chest. Her milky skin glowed iridescently against the deep bronze tone of his firm, muscular flesh. They seemed beautiful together. The perfect contrast. The perfect balance.

He carried her to the bed and arranged her on the sheets, then he lay beside her. His gaze melted over her. "I want to touch you everywhere," he murmured.

The strokes of his fingertips alternated. First he was light as a mountain breeze. Then he claimed her flesh, massaging deeply. "You're so soft," he said. "Your skin. It's like satin."

He pinched her nipples between his fingertips and rolled the sensitive nubs. Tingling excitement spread through her body.

She reached down and held him, gradually increasing the pressure of her grasp until he exhaled a moan of passion. "Don't stop."

But his expression, at the edge of ecstasy, was so beautiful that she paused. Nearly overwhelmed, she marveled at his dark radiance, the flash of his white teeth and his deep ebony eyes. His body was well-defined perfection. Lean and strong.

"Make love to me, Mace. Now."

He carefully spread her thighs, hooking his legs over hers. Their gazes locked as he stroked her, preparing her gently, making sure she was moist and ready for him.

"Now," she demanded. "Now."

"First this." He leaned over the edge of the bed, fished around in his trousers and came up with a condom.

"Of course," she said. She wasn't thinking about protection, but he was. Mace would always do the right thing. She could trust him to never hurt her.

He rose above her, supporting himself on his elbows, careful not to put his entire weight on her body. Never had there been a more considerate and skillful lover.

When he entered her, hard and strong, she erupted in a burst of desire, hot as a lava flow. Again and again, he thrust. She shuddered as brilliant, cataclysmic starbursts rocked her world.

Making love with him was everything she hoped for and more. She couldn't believe it. Again and again she was surprised by one climax after another.

Lovemaking had never been like this before. She'd always held back, fearful of losing control. With Mace she abandoned all restraint. She cried his name and clawed at his back like a wild creature. She was driven, consumed by desire.

Finally, when their passion was spent, they collapsed side by side on the bed.

The very expensive dinner in the other room was getting cold, but she didn't care. Nothing mattered except the man who stretched out beside her. Her hero.

His head turned toward her. All the tension had left his face. He looked completely relaxed. ''I'd say this was worth the trip to Denver.''

''Oh, yes.''

''You know I'll always take good care of you.''

''I know.'' And she believed him. All the misfortunes in her life faded away. Her future was sunlight and honey, bright and sweet.

She was surprised to find an appetite for dinner. The food she'd ordered was better than anything she'd eaten before. She felt as if she could savor each individual ingredient.

Quite possibly the charm of their dinner was heightened by their nudity. There seemed to be no need for clothing.

Other times when she'd made love, Nicole couldn't wait to get dressed and hide herself. With Mace she felt unselfconscious and natural. She enjoyed the way he'd reach over and casually touch her hair, and it was a sheer pleasure to watch him, to admire his body. She felt sexy and innocent at the same time.

''Tomorrow,'' he said, ''we're going to meet Blake Wentworth for lunch at one o'clock.''

''Ugh! That sounds like a recipe for indigestion. Do I have to come along?''

"I'm not letting you out of my sight," he promised. "Especially not while we're in Denver."

She liked his concern for her safety. "You're so different from anybody I've ever known."

"I can say the same about you." He chuckled.

She dabbed at the corners of her mouth with a linen napkin. "What's so funny?"

"I'm always amused by the way you eat. So prim and proper. It's especially cute while you're naked."

She arched an eyebrow. "Did you want me to get dressed?"

"Hell, no."

As soon as they finished dessert, he jumped her. They were rowdy as a couple of kids, making love again and again, until they fell into a blissfully exhausted sleep.

THE NEXT MORNING Nicole woke to find him staring at her. She smiled lazily. "What time is it?"

"Almost eleven o'clock. The way I figure, we've got just enough time to make love in the shower before we meet Blake."

"Sounds like a plan." She stretched and yawned, flinging an arm across his torso. "Last night was the best time I've ever had in my whole life."

He hugged her, then sat up on the bed and unfastened his necklace. "I want you to have this."

She rubbed her eyes, trying to erase the surprise she felt. "Wasn't the bear a gift from Tata Charlie?"

"It's my most precious possession. Like you, it's something I'll never let out of my sight."

His words felt important, but she'd didn't understand why. "What are you saying?"

"I want you to be with me forever, Nicole. Will you marry me?"

"I can't." A sharp chill pierced her morning bliss. "I can't marry you, Mace. Because I'm still married to Derek."

Chapter Sixteen

His fingers closed tightly over the bear totem. The turquoise and silver beads felt cold in his hand. Mace had almost given his heart to a woman who lied to him once and was still lying. She had betrayed his trust in the worst way. *She was still married.*

He had no right to be in bed with her, no right to be thinking of her as his mate.

"You led me to believe," he said, "that you were divorced."

"I ran away from Derek," she said. "I was afraid to file for divorce, afraid he'd find me."

"You lied to me."

She sat up on the bed and pulled up the sheet to cover her nakedness. "I never said I was divorced."

"Maybe not in so many words, but—"

"Not in any words," she said.

Her blue eyes pleaded for understanding. They had worked so hard to develop trust. From his first interrogation, when she told him virtually nothing, to this latest evasion, they had run through every shade of trust and mistrust. She wasn't a liar, but she hadn't been honest with him. She couldn't be honest. There were secrets she always kept hidden in her heart.

"You should have told me," he said.

"Now you know."

She tossed her head, and her incredible blond hair tumbled over her shoulder. God, she was beautiful. Last night had been the fulfillment of a dream. The sheer physical pleasure of their lovemaking was unsurpassed in his experience.

But Mace needed more than great sex, and he doubted it was possible for Nicole to give herself completely and without reservation. There was always something she held back because of her fear, her abusive past or from habit.

"Please," she said. "You've got to trust me."

"You've got it backward, Nicole. You're the one who's incapable of trust. Your secrets stand between us."

He looked down at the necklace in his hand. Tata Charlie had given it to him when he came of age. It was a symbol of his manhood. A real man, a confident man, would forgive her. But Mace wasn't perfect.

Opening his hand, he allowed the polished silver to fall onto the bed between them.

The necklace should have been symbolic of a promise that he would always be there. He would always protect her. What a futile effort! "I can't save you from your past."

"Ask me anything," she said quickly. "Please, Mace, I'll tell you anything."

"We should be going." He rose from the bed and strode toward the bathroom. "We have a lunch date with Blake at one o'clock."

"Stop." She stood on the bed with the sheets pulled up to her chest. "This isn't fair. You don't respect me because of who I once was."

She'd gone on the attack. Her accusation was an arrow through his heart. "What are you saying?"

"You're just like everybody else." Her voice dripped with venom as she struck out at him. "You hate me."

"Nicole, I don't hate you."

"You think anybody who puts up with abuse is weak and pitiful. You think I liked being a trophy wife, but you can never know how hard my life has been." She dashed away a tear. "I allowed my husband to mistreat me. Not because I liked it. But because I was trapped. There was no escape."

"I believe you," he said. "But you've got to let it go. I don't want to spend the rest of my life rescuing you."

"I thought you wanted to protect me."

"You've got to rescue yourself first," he said. "You have to find the strength within yourself to conquer your fear."

Until then, Mace knew, there was no chance for a real, honest relationship. Until she felt safe within herself, there would always be lies and manipulation, even though she didn't mean to play games—just like she didn't mean to lash out at him—the pattern was there.

He turned away from her and entered the bathroom, closing the door quietly behind him. Damn it! How could she not mention that she was still married? There had been dozens of opportunities for her to tell him. Even when Daisy was joking around about catering their wedding, Nicole might have dropped in a mention that she wasn't, in fact, a single woman.

He turned on the shower and stepped under the spray, washing away the lingering scent of their passion. He loved her, and that wouldn't change. But there was no place for that love to grow because she wouldn't let him get close. Damn it!

Now he was mad. And that was exactly what she expected. In her book all men were bad. All men were abusers like her ex-husband…make that her *current* husband.

He finished his shower, toweled dry and rubbed a space in the steamed-up bathroom mirror to shave. As far as he was concerned, the ball was in her court. If she was ready to try a relationship with him, she had to take the first step with complete honesty, nothing held back. No blame.

Until then, they were friends. Nothing more.

Actually, he was also a sheriff. And he had a job to do while they were in Denver. He needed to get some answers from Blake Wentworth.

Mace exhaled and forced himself to overcome his emotional turmoil about Nicole, the woman he loved but might never have. His brain started working out another theory of the kidnapping and murder of Joey Wentworth.

FORTY-FIVE MINUTES LATER, Mace and Nicole strolled down the Sixteenth Street Mall in downtown Denver, headed for a Lower Downtown restaurant. She felt like she was walking in the past. Flustered. Frightened. Furious.

Mace said, "You already know my theory about Blake being involved in the kidnapping. He probably hired professional thugs to do the actual abduction and murder."

"Right."

She and Mace hadn't discussed their argument in

the hotel bedroom. Neither of them apologized or forgave. Now he was sounding off on another of his theories...as if last night had never happened.

"But pegging Blake as the mastermind doesn't explain everything," Mace said. "First, there was the mess at the cabin that made it look like a robbery."

"And the theft of my money," she added. Though she didn't want to talk about the crime, she wouldn't indulge in a childish silent treatment.

"The only one who could have tossed the cabin was Joey. The Feds did a thorough forensic investigation. They found no fingerprints, no mud from footprints, no fibers, no hairs. Nothing. Plus, professional thugs would know better than to break the bathroom window from the inside."

"I'll concede the point," she said coldly. If Mace intended to ignore the greatest passion in the history of the world, fine. If he wanted to pretend he didn't propose, fine. "Joey messed up the cabin. So what?"

"Here's another piece of evidence. Throughout this kidnapping, the ransom delivery and the aftermath, the kidnappers focused on you. But the thugs didn't know you. Nor does Blake. The only person who would insist on your involvement had to be Joey."

She halted on the sidewalk, glaring. "So, you still think Joey instigated his own kidnapping."

"He worked out the details with his uncle, who hired the professionals. The motive for the Wentworth boys—Joey and Blake—was to get their hands on a share of that ransom money."

"Much as I hate to burst your bright red balloon," she said, "Joey's dead. Did he plan that, too?"

"Something went wrong," Mace said. "They had to get rid of him."

Though he faced her, Mace didn't make eye contact. His attitude was distant and uninvolved. And she didn't know how to deal with this behavior. In her experience an argument usually meant violence followed by apology. Making up was the bonus.

But Mace hadn't hit her or even threatened her. Instead of responding to her own anger, he walked away. Well, fine. She was the expert at stonewalling. As soon as she picked up her stuff in Elkhorn, she'd be gone.

He started walking again, leaving her to catch up with him. "The restaurant is two blocks up. An Italian place."

Nicole assessed the restaurant with a professional eye. Nice decor. Well-stocked bar. The clientele seemed to be mainly professional people in business suits. It wouldn't be a bad place to work.

Mace requested a table by the window so they could watch for Blake. She perused the menu, deciding on fettuccine Alfredo and a calamari appetizer. When the waitress asked for their drink order, Nicole asked for a sweet merlot.

"An orange soda for me," Mace said.

"No wine?"

"I'm working," he said.

She carefully placed her napkin on her lap. "I suppose that means our vacation is over."

"I'm not opposed to conversation."

And so they talked about the weather and the Broncos and how much Denver had grown. It was the sort of impersonal chat she might have had on a bus. Though she longed to say something more probing and personal, Nicole held herself in check.

She wouldn't give him the satisfaction. He was the

one who rejected her, after all. He accused her of lying. He didn't think she was good enough, pure enough, perfect enough for him.

Halfway through the meal, Mace excused himself and put in a call to Blake on his cell phone. While he talked, she watched him surreptitiously, searching for a sign that he regretted what had happened.

He disconnected the call. "Blake isn't going to make it to lunch. He wants us to meet him at his home in southwest Denver at five o'clock."

"Then I guess we'll be spending another night in Denver," she said.

Their gazes met across the table. Sparks flew. She knew they were both remembering last night's passionate lovemaking, their naked bodies entwined in the sheets. They'd been joined as one.

"We'll drive back tonight," Mace said. "I'll use the rental car."

"I don't mind staying," she said. If he gave her another night, their differences might be resolved. There were very few problems between a man and a woman that couldn't be solved by great sex.

"That's not the answer," he said tersely. A muscle in his jaw twitched.

"I'm not following," she said. "What was the question?"

"Think about it, Nicole."

She threw up her hands. "Why does this have to be so complicated? Why can't we have a good time with each other and then…"

"Move on? Run away?" He shook his head. "I want more from you. A lifetime of commitment and trust. I want you to believe in yourself as much as you believe in me or anybody else. Then you can answer the question I asked this morning.''

Will you marry me?

The unspoken words hung between them. If she gave a quick yes, she'd betray him and herself as well. Before she promised to love and honor him, Nicole must come to terms with her fear. Not a simple task. ''I can't figure this out in a few minutes.''

He reached across the table, clasped her hand and lightly squeezed her fingers. ''I'm a patient man.''

All her life she'd waited for a man like Mace—a man who cared enough about her to do the right thing. But what was the right thing? Where should she start in taking charge of her life? ''My mother said that good things were worth working for.''

And that was what Nicole intended to do. She'd figure this out. She couldn't stand to lose him.

After their lunch, they had time to kill before driving out to Blake's house. Since they were already in LoDo, Nicole suggested, ''There was a gallery in this area where Joey displayed. Let's find it.''

Meandering through the refurbished brick buildings and cobblestone pathways, they located the gallery. In the front window was a landscape of mesas and mountains that Nicole recognized immediately. ''Joey did that.''

When they stepped inside, the proprietor glanced at them, then did a double take. He gaped at Nicole. ''Oh my God! You're Joey's muse.''

''I am?''

''I've handled four paintings where you are the central figure. Plus one on commission.'' He crowded close to her. ''You don't happen to have more of

Joey's work, do you? Since his murder, his art has become very, very lucrative.''

She thought of his studio at the cabin, crammed full of artwork. Joey had been struggling for years, trying to get noticed. Now, by dying, he'd brought his career to life.

''Tell me about the commissioned painting,'' Mace said.

''It was paid for about a month ago, and I blush to tell you how cheaply. A highly specific request.''

''Go on,'' Nicole said.

''It was a painting of you.'' He beamed at Nicole. ''Not a very flattering setting. A graveyard. And you were supposed to be a monster with a black heart.''

She gasped. Joey's painting wasn't a reflection of his own feelings for her. He didn't hate her. But apparently someone else did. ''Who commissioned it?''

''I really can't say.''

Mace produced his badge. ''If necessary, I'll be back with a subpoena.''

The proprietor rolled his eyes. ''I suppose it's all right to tell you. Now that Joey is dead.'' He leaned toward them and whispered conspiratorially, ''It was Joey's uncle, Blake Wentworth.''

Nicole didn't understand. Blake didn't even know her. ''Did Joey know that Blake commissioned the painting?''

''He did not,'' said the proprietor. ''His uncle made me promise not to tell him. I think Blake wanted to slip his nephew some cash and give him encouragement at the same time.''

She left the gallery more confused than when they entered. On the drive out to Blake's house, she began to draw some scary conclusions. "What if Blake commissioned that painting as a front for someone else?"

Mace nodded but said nothing.

There was only one person who hated her that much, only one man who would want a painting of her with a cold, dead, black heart.

MACE CHECKED THE ADDRESS twice before he parked in front of Blake's house—a pleasant two-story frame house in a relatively new suburb. Mace had expected a more lavish homestead for the CEO of Wentworth Oil Exploration.

"What do you think?" he asked Nicole. "You're familiar with the habits of the rich and famous. Is this the right house for Blake Wentworth?"

"Not at all. I know he's supporting his family in another household, but I'd expect more."

"His money problems might be worse than we thought."

As he went up the sidewalk with her, Mace sensed danger. He glanced at the barren October lawns in this quiet neighborhood, then looked up and down the street. There seemed to be no tangible reason for his concern. Yet, he felt edgy. If he'd been in Elkhorn, he'd call Barry for backup.

He took the cell phone from his jacket pocket and held it. If he contacted the Denver PD and this turned out to be nothing, Mace came out looking like a jerk.

"What are you doing?" she asked.

"Being a good cop."

He'd be more the fool if he ignored potential danger. Talking to one of his buddies downtown, he requested backup. "There's no immediate threat, but I wouldn't mind if you'd send by a patrol car. No sirens.''

He disconnected and turned to Nicole. "Maybe you should stay in the car.''

"I won't let fear run my life.''

Swell, now she was taking his advice. "I'm asking you to be prudent.''

But she charged up the sidewalk and pressed the doorbell.

The door was answered by a young man in neat blue jeans and a button-down shirt. "Come in,'' he said. "He's waiting for you.''

"Who are you?'' Mace asked.

"Call me Jimbo.''

"Okay, Jimbo.'' That was one of the names Joey had written in his sketchpad. When the number was traced, Jimbo had answered from a public phone at the airport. A professional criminal from out of town?

"Come in,'' Jimbo said.

Mace didn't like the setup. He reached under his jacket and unfastened the snap on his belt holster so he could pull his automatic in quick-draw fashion.

Jimbo escorted them into a study and closed the door. Another man stood by the door and a third was seated in a brown leather chair opposite a large oak desk.

"Derek!'' Nicole's voice was high pitched, resonant with terror.

"Surprise, surprise.''

Derek Brewer, Nicole's husband, pushed away from the desk and stood. He was a big man, expensively dressed, with thinning brown hair. Mace noticed his flat, blue eyes, utterly devoid of expression.

They were the eyes of a cold-blooded killer. "Where's Blake?"

"Tied up at the moment." Derek shared a laugh with his buddies before he instructed Jimbo to take Mace's gun from the holster.

Mace didn't object. He knew backup was on the way. All he had to do was keep Derek talking. "So you're behind the kidnapping and the extortion. How'd you pull this off?"

"Why don't you tell me, Sheriff. From what I understand, you're the man with the theories."

"Somewhere you saw one of Joey's paintings of Nicole," Mace said. "In Blake's office?"

"Good guess. Blake isn't exactly in my league." He stared at Nicole. "You remember, don't you? Guys like Blake Wentworth were beneath me."

She said nothing.

Derek continued, "My law firm was coming after Wentworth Oil Exploration for nonpayment of debt. When I saw the picture, Blake told me all about his idiot nephew and the girl who was staying with him in Elkhorn." Derek turned toward Nicole and sneered. "That would be you."

Her voice quavered. "Why did you involve anyone else? It would have been enough to come after me."

"But not nearly so much fun. Since Blake and Joey both needed money, I suggested the kidnapping. They were happy to go along with the program. Can you tell me why, Sheriff?"

"Whether they got the money from Joey's closed trust fund or ripped off the insurance company, they figured it was really their money, anyway." Mace added, "Neither of them is crooked."

"Which was why neither of them added up the

numbers. They really believed I'd share the ransom."
Derek shook his head in disbelief. "Why would I? I
hired the pros. I paid for the arrangements, including
that beat-up Jeep Wagoneer that we exploded. Why
would I give my hard-earned money to the Wentworths?"

"That's why you killed Joey," Mace asked. "To
keep his share."

"A business decision," Derek said. "And I figured
Blake would be placated by the life insurance payout
on his nephew. Unfortunately, Uncle Blake seems to
have gotten an attack of conscience."

"You were the person he called from Elkhorn,"
Mace said. "On the untraceable cell phone."

"That self-righteous jerk was stupid to call me."

"He yelled at you," Mace said. He glanced toward
the window, hoping he'd see a patrol car.

"Both of the Wentworths were weak links," Derek
said. He placed his two fists together and yanked them
apart as if snapping an invisible chain.

Nicole gasped as she watched the implied violence,
but she found her voice. "You'll never get away with
this."

"I'm above the law, Nicole. I want you to understand that." He came around the desk quickly and
stood before her. "Men like me can do anything they
want. Nobody can stop me."

"Don't touch her," Mace said. If Derek hurt her,
he wouldn't be able to hold himself in check.

"You can't stop me." Derek turned toward Mace
and thrust out his chest. "She's my wife. My property. I can do anything to her that I want."

"Not anymore," she said with surprising strength
in her voice. "You can't hurt me. Not anymore."

"Shut up," he snarled. "Okay, kids. Here's what happens next. We bring Blake in here, and we make it look like he shot Mace and then committed suicide. The Feds and the cops assume that Blake ordered the kidnapping. And this is over."

He nodded to Jimbo, who left the room, presumably to get Blake. Mace glanced toward the other man who stood near the door, watching disinterestedly. Though he was certainly armed, the gun wasn't in his hand.

"What happens to me?" Nicole demanded.

"You return to the arms of your loving husband. That would be me. And you do whatever I say for the rest of your natural life. Or until I get bored with you."

"I'd rather die," she said.

"That could be arranged," he said in a flat monotone. "A very slow, painful death. It could take weeks, months. You know how I handle disobedience, Nicole. Don't push me."

"I won't obey you."

Though Mace applauded her refusal to be bullied, now was not the time. Backup was on the way. "Settle down," he cautioned.

"You were right, Mace. I won't run my life with fear. Never again will I run away." She stood tall, straight and beautiful. "Sure, I'm scared. Real scared. But fear doesn't tell me what to do, because I believe in stronger feelings. I believe in myself."

The fire of courage shone in her eyes. He'd never been so proud. She spoke to him in a steady, calm, quiet tone. "The answer to your question is yes. Mace, I want to make a commitment for all the right reasons. Because I love you."

Her words echoed in the small room. The raw strength of her conviction encouraged him. They wouldn't die. Not now. He and Nicole had everything to live for. "And I love you."

Derek stepped between them. "Isn't that cute? The backwoods sheriff and the waitress." He laughed. "Give it up, Nicole. He can't rescue you this time."

"He doesn't need to," she said.

Derek scoffed. "Really?"

"Because I can rescue myself."

Derek drew back his hand to strike her.

With a feral cry, Nicole sprang at him with arms flailing.

Mace had to make his move. He charged the guy by the door and grabbed the gun from his hand. One hard, adrenaline-fueled uppercut and the guy went down.

Mace pivoted, gun in hand. It was a .22 caliber, accurate at close range.

Derek held Nicole by the throat. "I could snap her neck in—"

Mace fired twice. There was no time for a standoff and an exchange of empty threats. One bullet hit Derek's shoulder. The other buried in his kneecap.

His leg buckled. When he fell, his grasp on Nicole loosened, and she struggled free.

Nicole flew into Mace's arms as the front door burst open and the backup cops raced inside. Mace hardly noticed the commotion as Derek and his henchmen were taken into custody. His entire field of vision was filled with the sight of her lovely face.

She stepped away from him and picked up her purse. Reaching inside, she pulled out the turquoise and silver necklace, which she held toward him. "I'm ready to wear this now."

"Turn around, Nicole."

He lifted her braid and fastened the necklace around her throat. In his heart they were betrothed, and he would never lose sight of her again.

* * * * *

If you liked
RESTLESS SPIRIT,
you'll love Cassie Miles's next
Harlequin Intrigue,
PROTECTING THE INNOCENT,

coming to you July 2004.
Don't miss it!

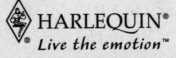

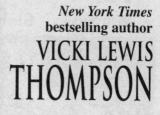
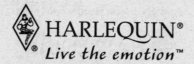

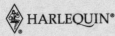

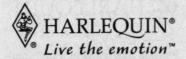

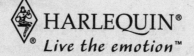

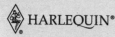

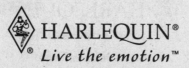

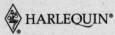

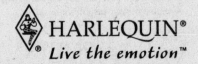